PAYBACKS

Visit us at www.boldstrokesbooks.com

What Reviewers Say About Gabrielle Goldsby's Fiction

"Such a Pretty Face [is] a delightful read with solid storytelling and engaging characters. The reader is immediately drawn into one woman's journey of self-discovery...Mia's story...is written with deep emotion and Goldsby brings the reader into her painful transformation...deftly." – *Lambda Book Report*

In *Such a Pretty Face* "...Goldsby, skillfully mixing sharp humor and incisive insight, sorts out...emotional issues with solid plotting—and plenty of hot sex on the side." – *Q Syndicate*

"Child molestation, blazing gunplay, menacing double-crosses, ruthless cover-ups, a suspect suicide, sleazy cop corruption, and trafficking in young children—this is one gritty police procedural. Detective Foster Everett is battling alcohol and relationship demons, not getting along with her female superior, and uneasy being a dyke in a macho office. She and her supportive male partner become enmeshed in a stomach-churning case involving the filming and distribution of kiddie porn, a situation that reaches into the highest ranks of the police department—and runs right into the fabled "wall of silence" that shields law enforcement misdeeds. Goldsby's zip-quick novel is packed with a multidimensional cast of complex characters, most prominently lesbian bar bouncer Riley Meideros, an aloof woman with unexpected emotional depth for whom Foster inevitably falls. The romance element sizzles with its own tension, but the crackling appeal of this gripping mystery lies in how ably Goldsby depicts unsettling sex crimes and immoral police conduct." – *Q Syndicate*

"If you like cop stories, this one should be at the top of your 2008 reading list. It's just terrific." – *Lesbian News*

"Wall of Silence is a cracking good read." – *L-Word.com*

"The novel is perfectly plotted and has a very real voice and consistently accurate tone, which is not always the case with lesbian mysteries." – *Midwest Book Review*

By the Author

Such a Pretty Face

Wall of Silence, Second Edition

Remember Tomorrow

The Caretaker's Daughter (Ebook)

Never Wake (Ebook)

Paybacks

PAYBACKS

by
Gabrielle Goldsby

2009

PAYBACKS

ISBN 10: 1-60282-046-5
ISBN 13: 978-1-60282-046-3

THIS TRADE PAPERBACK ORIGINAL IS PUBLISHED BY
BOLD STROKES BOOKS, INC.
P.O. BOX 249
VALLEY FALLS, NY 12185

FIRST EDITION: JANUARY 2009

CREDITS
EDITORS: CINDY CRESAP AND STACIA SEAMAN
PRODUCTION DESIGN: STACIA SEAMAN
COVER DESIGN BY SHERI (GRAPHICARTIST2020@HOTMAIL.COM)

Acknowledgments

The nucleus of *Paybacks*, the Matinee Book you are holding, began as a 1,000 word challenge on a popular fan fiction site. I was amazed at the number of readers who wrote in insisting that they wanted to know more about these two characters. At their request, I happily wrote three more small vignettes before I came up against a wall. Namely, the characters began to outgrow the format I was using to tell their story. Years passed, and I was lucky enough to be a published author with Bold Strokes Books when the description of the Matinee Book line came to my attention.

I immediately thought of *Paybacks* and how I had been unable to tell the story I wanted to in the short story format. With the encouragement of my publisher, the early assistance of my beta readers Mechael W and Nikki G, and the indispensible help of my editors Cindy Cresap and Stacia Seaman, I was finally able to tell the full story.

To the readers who wrote to me years after the originals were posted, thank you for your continued interest. Novelization from short story often requires major changes in format. In this case a name change was necessary, but rest assured these are the same two characters. I did not use any of the material from the original short stories, but the original intent—that being sex and revenge—is still there. I hope you enjoy.

Gabrielle

Dedication

To the readers who, years later,
still wanted to read the whole story.

Chapter One

Roheibeth High School Ten-Year Class Reunion

It was, Colby thought, a good plan. Right up until her clit started twitching. As soon as that happened, she should have forgotten about exorcising old demons and instead walked the hell out of her ten-year high school reunion. She was fairly well off, had owned her own business since graduating from college, and had reinvented herself both mentally and physically. What did she care if these people knew how well she had turned out? She'd been there for over an hour and not one of them had approached her. Oh, she could see them whispering behind their hands, trying to place her face. She even thought one of them, a short, squat guy with freckles on his nude scalp, and glasses that looked like they had come in a two-for-one deal, figured out who she was.

Colby didn't mind that she wasn't recognized or approached. The woman with the asymmetrical haircut, short little black dress, and matching stilettos looked very different from the long-haired, skinny, but painfully out of shape girl of ten years ago. Colby didn't think she had worn a dress or a skirt until her sophomore year in college, which was why she loved wearing them now. It made her feel as if she were putting on a disguise. Not that a disguise was needed at her ten-year reunion. If asked a week after graduation, she doubted any of these people could have successfully picked Colby Dennis out of a lineup.

Colby had hidden in a dark corner of the room where she could put her back to the wall and watch as people she barely recognized filed nervously into the gym. The clit twitching had begun the instant a striking dark-haired woman wearing a white shirt and black pants appeared in the entryway. Colby recognized her own arousal incredulously. *That's just perfect. Nothing for months and then I go hyperaware at the sight of Mackenzie Brandt, of all people?* Colby ignored her instinct to hide behind hair that had been cut off years ago, and instead stared openly.

The photo she had been given of Mackenzie Brandt had not done her justice. A photo could not show how confident she looked when she leaned down to give her name to the woman at the badge table. A photo could not possibly make Colby's heart race up her throat as it did when Mackenzie smiled and reached for her name-tag. Mackenzie said something to the wife of their old high school class president before obediently pressing the sticker onto her shirt just above her full breasts. *Jesus, take the wheel! How could I have forgotten those?* Colby remembered Mackenzie's chest being smaller than her own. By no means had she been flat chested, but she had been far from the perfect handful Colby was looking at now. *Perfect handful? What the...? Remember who you're dealing with and why you're here.*

Mackenzie smiled and talked to people who approached, but she never fully integrated into any one group. Occasionally, Mackenzie would lift her head and scan the room as if she were either looking for someone or had somehow sensed she was being observed. Colby tightened her jaw, pushed away from the wall, then abruptly stopped moving when Mackenzie looked right at her. The smile that had been on Mackenzie's face the whole time Colby had been watching her disappeared almost completely. Colby's pulse hammered at her throat as she locked eyes with the only person in the room she hoped remembered her. Even from the small distance Colby saw Mackenzie's face darken. *Blushing?* Not the Mackenzie she remembered. Colby recognized her arousal despite not having felt it so fiercely in a very long time. Mackenzie made no move to approach, but based on reaction alone, it was obvious she had recognized her. The plan, if she had ever really had one, was out the window. This didn't feel like she'd expected it would. Where was the anger? The righteous indignation?

"Colby Dennis? I can't believe you of all people came to this farce!"

Colby reluctantly tore her attention from Mackenzie to look down into a pair of jubilant green eyes. The bright red hair was new, but the mischievous expression was the only hint Colby needed to recognize Lara Coulter, her high school lab partner and fellow member of the unpopular crowd.

"That's a great dress, Colby. You got the surgery too?"

"The surgery?" Colby looked down at her breasts. "No, they're mine."

"They are?" Lara moved closer to Colby and peered into her cleavage. "Nice, but that's not what I meant. LASIK, right? Isn't it the best not to have to wear the bifocals anymore?"

"Yeah, fantastic." Colby craned her neck to find Mackenzie again, but she had moved to some other part of the room.

Colby turned back to Lara and felt the tension ease from her as she realized how much and how little her friend had changed. Lara's flair for the dramatic had seemingly increased with age. She wore her bright red hair high atop her head. Her hairstyle was complemented by long daisy earrings of varying colors. Miraculously, Lara had managed to find a dress that had almost all the colors of her earrings. Her hair had been a dramatic black in high school, as had her eye shadow and lips. As the only Goth student in the class, Lara had always stood out.

Colby had never understood why someone would invite that. Her only wish had been to blend in, get through, and then get out without getting noticed. For the most part, she had been successful—except where Mackenzie Brandt had been concerned.

Colby bent down for the "straight-girl body-separate hug," but Lara threw her arms around her and kissed her square on the mouth. Colby blinked and stepped back. "What was that?"

Lara shrugged. "I always wondered what it would be like to kiss a woman, and you're one of the few lesbians I know."

Colby frowned. "How do you know I'm a lesbian?"

Lara's expressive eyebrows arched, and Colby realized she had dyed those too. "You mean you aren't?"

Colby sighed. "Of course I am, but how did you...?"

A movement out of the corner of her eye caused Colby to turn. Mackenzie was standing a few feet away with a strange look on her face. Had she seen Lara kiss her? So what if she had? Colby felt trapped by some question to which she didn't know the answer. She remembered a similar feeling in high school on the few occasions she actually had conversations with Mackenzie. To her great relief, someone stepped in front of Mackenzie and the contact was broken.

"Whoa, you used to hate gym. Now you look like you live in one."

"What? Oh yeah, I work out a little."

"Uh-huh, a little. I can barely get through *Three Minute Abs*. I like what you've done with your hair. That asymmetrical looks great on you, but you could do with a few highlights here and there. Here's my card. You live in Portland, right?" Colby nodded. "I take walk-ins. When are you heading home?"

"I haven't decided yet. I thought about staying through the weekend."

"Staying in Roheibeth? What the hell for? I'm driving back to Portland first thing in the morning."

Colby would have given the answer she had given her staff about needing a vacation, but her attention had already gravitated back to Mackenzie. She remembered Mackenzie as a menacing figure and had certainly never thought she would turn into this beautiful woman. Colby recognized the smile. It had never been directed toward her, but the way she looked, the way she tilted her head while listening, and even the whiteness of her teeth were familiar now. It was as if all the years dropped away and they were back in high school.

"Damn, she looks good," Colby said softly.

Lara followed her gaze to the couple having what appeared to be an intimate conversation in the center of the room.

"Yes, she does."

Colby looked at Lara and back toward Mackenzie. "Looks like that guy is already moving in for the kill."

"Isn't he wasting his time? I always thought she was gay too."

Colby didn't look at Lara when she answered. "She's married."

"Really? You sure she's not gay?"

Not even remotely sure. Colby struggled to keep annoyance from her face. How had Lara picked up on something like that when she hadn't? It wasn't so much that she had thought Mackenzie was straight in high school. She never thought Mackenzie capable of having relationships at all, unless smirking, shoving, and glaring were involved. Ten years ago there were two types of kids at Roheibeth High: those who bullied and those who carried lunch money in both pockets to increase the odds of being left with enough to buy a bag of chips. Mackenzie Brandt was her bully, her tormenter, the one person she had been unable to push to the far reaches of her memory even ten years later.

"Boy, did she have it bad for you," Lara said.

"Me? I'm the reason she got expelled, remember? She hated me, and the feeling was mutual."

"Well, it looks like you're about to get the chance to discuss that mutual feeling. She's on her way over."

Any response Colby would have made froze on her tongue.

Mackenzie was indeed on her way over. Her direct gaze left no doubt for anyone watching her that she had a purpose in mind, and that was to get to Colby.

"Okay. It was great seeing you. Don't be a stranger. Bye-bye, now."

Colby turned to tell Lara to stay, but she had already disappeared into the knot of drunken swaying people.

Colby looked off to the right, smiled, nodded to someone she didn't know, and tried to act like she wasn't shocked by how badly her pulse was racing. Why was she so afraid? It had been so long and things had changed. She had changed. She was no longer a skinny/fat teenager caught in the grasp of a much stronger, impossibly tall aggressor.

"Colby. Hello, you probably don't remember me, but—"

"I remember you," Colby said and was surprised at how cold she sounded. Mackenzie's face blanched as she continued. "Do you really believe ten years was enough time for me to forget how you made my life hell?"

Mackenzie winced. "That's…not what I meant."

"Oh, well maybe you thought I had forgotten how terrified I was to come to school, thanks to you?"

"I didn't think that either. I hoped you would let me explain."

Someone bumped into Colby, sending punch sloshing over the rim of her glass as she lurched forward. Mackenzie grasped each of her biceps to steady her. The rebuke froze on Colby's lips, stopped cold by the glare Mackenzie was sending to whoever had bumped into her. Colby thought she heard a sheepish apology, and Mackenzie, apparently appeased, looked down. She seemed surprised to find her hands were still on Colby's arms, yet didn't remove them for another few seconds.

"Sorry."

Colby would have asked "what for?" if she had been able to speak. Her face flushed about the time the rest of her body did. This wasn't supposed to be how it went. She was supposed to confront Mackenzie about the crappy things she had done to her. She was supposed to revel in the knowledge she was no longer the weakling skinny/fat kid she once was; instead, she was acting like a love-struck teenager. *No, no, no—not love-struck. Poor choice of words.*

"Can we go somewhere and talk? Just for a few minutes? Please?"

Colby studied the earnest-looking woman in front of her and came up with four biting comments—none of which came out of her mouth.

The "please" was what got her. Colby would have never imagined she would hear Mackenzie Brandt say that word to anyone, let alone to her. Mackenzie bit the edge of her bottom lip. A small, innocent gesture and one Colby probably wouldn't have noticed if they hadn't had to stand so close in order to be heard over the loud music.

A familiar thought needled its way into Colby's conscious mind. *Her eyes are black. If they aren't black, they're the darkest brown I've ever seen.*

"I'll give you two minutes," Colby said sternly. "But I think you're wasting your time."

Mackenzie's sigh was audible. "How about in there?" she asked.

Colby followed Mackenzie's gaze to the door leading to the girls' locker room, and the fine hairs on her arms stood up. She had to be kidding. Could she have forgotten that the locker room was the last place they had seen each other before all hell broke loose? Was this some kind of fucked-up form of adult bullying? Act like you don't know you're bringing up bad memories to mess with the other person's head?

Fine, if she wanted to play, they could do that. Colby nodded and walked swiftly toward the locker room. *She has no fucking idea who she's playing with.*

❖

Colby pushed through the swinging doors of the locker room, turned, and waited, arms folded, legs braced. Mackenzie walked into the room and stopped abruptly upon finding Colby standing just a few feet into the room.

"Say what you need to say," Colby said, pleased she sounded steadier than she felt.

"First, I wanted to tell you how gorgeous you look."

Colby's mouth would have dropped open if shock hadn't fused it in place. What the fuck was that? A compliment? "Did you ask me in here to get my beauty tips?"

"No, I...I..."

Again with the blush? And what was with that stuttering? This woman was good, really good.

"I didn't think you would come to something like this."

Colby had changed her mind about attending the reunion at least half a dozen times. At the last minute, she had rented a car and driven the three hours from Portland. She had been given an all-expense-paid opportunity to prove Mackenzie Brandt wrong. She was successful, not a "little nobody," as she had overheard Mackenzie say to one of her friends.

She had left this town and made something of herself. She was no longer the scared little nerd hiding behind her hair in the back of the classroom. She wanted to rub all this in Mackenzie Brandt's face, and if she could get a little dirt on her in the process, then all the better.

The problem was, the woman standing in front of her seemed nothing like the girl she had known. Oh, the resemblance was there, only the thick dark hair wasn't pulled back into a severe ponytail or cornrows, and Mackenzie's high school uniform of baggy jeans and sweatshirts would be a travesty on such a fit-looking body. But this was still Mackenzie Brandt, the girl who had shoved her into lockers as an afterthought and who had called her both skinny and fat before settling on the painfully accurate skinny/fat.

A shiver ran through Colby. She rubbed her arms for warmth.

Mackenzie's eyes followed the motion, settling briefly on Colby's breasts before returning to her face. It wouldn't be the first time Colby had caught a straight woman appraising her breasts. But the look she recognized briefly on Mackenzie's face had nothing to do with sizing up a perceived opponent's attributes.

Desire. If she had harbored any doubts about Mackenzie's sexuality before, she no longer did. Her nipples became painfully hard, and her skimpy underwear would have to be removed if she hoped to be comfortable for the rest of the evening. *So that's it? All it takes to get me revved up is some bitch from my past to glance at me sideways? That's just great.*

"I'm here, and your two minutes are almost over," Colby said defensively.

"I'm so sorry for how I treated you when we were kids."

Shock left Colby speechless. She hadn't expected such a quick, and what looked to be heartfelt, apology. "We weren't kids. I was seventeen. You were what, nineteen?"

"No, we're the same age. I may be a few months older, but—"

It was Colby's turn to stutter. "I heard that you—"

"Had been held back? You believed that rumor?" Mackenzie smiled. "It was a lie. Before my parents moved us here, we lived close to the Tijuana border. Fake IDs were easy to come by, and the drinking age was eighteen in Tijuana." Mackenzie shrugged. "The way I made friends fast was by buying cigarettes for people. If any of the cashiers asked, I told them I'd been held back. Word got around, and people just assumed I was some badass delinquent who had missed a few grades while in juvi. I just went with it."

"You...went with it? So you're..."

"Twenty-eight, just like you."

"I'm twenty-seven." Colby glared her warning.

Mackenzie mock scowled in return, but managed to make it seem cute and playful. "Okay, you win. I'm older."

What the fuck was that? Are we playing with each other now? No, it wasn't playing; it was flirting. Mackenzie Brandt was flirting with her, and she was responding. No way was this happening. No way. "Okay, that's it. Your time is up. Nice seeing you and all that stuff."

Colby brushed past Mackenzie and was about to head out the door when a hand on her forearm stopped her. Colby yanked her arm away as if touched by a hot prong. She spun around, her fist up in a warning more than any real intention to strike out. "Don't you dare touch me. I hit back these days." She spat the words out with more venom than the gentle hold on her arm warranted. Mackenzie stumbled back. She couldn't have looked more shocked if Colby had popped her one for emphasis.

"Never. I would never hit you," Mackenzie said and her words sounded so fiercely possessive that Colby felt disoriented and confused. "Colby, I didn't mean anything by this. I just wanted you to give me a chance to tell you how very sorry I am for the things I did to you back then."

"Fine, you've told me. You feel better now?"

Mackenzie nibbled at the inside of her bottom lip. Colby soothed her own bottom lip with the tip of her tongue in sympathy and became angry when she realized she was doing it.

"No, I don't."

"Sorry to hear that. I'm sure there are people you could pay to listen to you explain about your fucked-up childhood. I, on the other hand, have no interest." When pain appeared briefly on Mackenzie's face, Colby refused to care.

"I'd like to make amends if possible."

"It's been years. What difference does it make now?" Colby studied Mackenzie carefully. The honest eyes, earnest face, even her height seemed different from what she remembered. But there was a familiarity that contrasted drastically with the nervousness emanating from this woman. She didn't remember teenaged Mackenzie being afraid of anything. Not that they had exactly known each other.

"I don't know. I just feel like I should."

"After ten years? What's wrong with you?" Colby asked.

"Let me guess. You've had a near-death experience, so now you're on one of those self-improvement quests where you have to apologize to all the people you've wronged in the past."

Mackenzie looked shocked and then she laughed. Colby almost laughed too, but was stunned silent by one traitorous thought. *I would never get tired of hearing her laugh.*

"Not exactly. Let's just say I have someone in my life who makes me want to be a better person and makes me regret a lot of the decisions I made in my youth."

"Must be a very special person." *Special, rich, and a man,* Colby thought bitterly. Mackenzie Brandt was a fool. She was no more straight than Colby herself. The Copelands were right; Mackenzie should have never married their son.

Mackenzie smiled and shrugged, and the pride and devotion in that smile made Colby feel petty and strange. When they were younger she had been certain her revenge would be that Mackenzie would end up alone in a shack somewhere, while she would end up popular and with a family. Instead, Colby knew she worked too hard and barely had a social life. Hell, socializing aside, she hadn't had sex in over six months, and even then it hadn't been good. Maybe that's what this was all about. She was horny and disappointed Mackenzie seemed more well balanced than she was.

"I can tell you still hate me, and I don't want that between us."

"What do you care? I don't live here anymore."

Colby would have preferred for Mackenzie to have flashed back in anger, but her voice was calm and her eyes steady when she answered. "I care enough to try to make things better between us. I care more than you'll ever know. I always have."

"Prove it," Colby said, shocking Mackenzie and shocking the breath from her own chest.

"How?"

"I don't know. You're the one who says you care. Prove to me how much." Where in the hell was she going with this? The shocked look on Mackenzie's face was slowly changing into something else. The desire she had so quickly hidden was now back. She focused on Colby's lips as she moved forward slowly.

"Is it okay if…?"

Colby blinked. Why in the hell would she? Her order that Mackenzie not touch her came flooding back. She would have to rescind that order if she wanted to see how far this unexpected attraction would go. Colby sighed and gave one nod of her head. Before she could even close her eyes Mackenzie's lips were there, pressing against hers, urging them open. The strength that had always scared her was being used to crush her to Mackenzie's torso.

Colby went limp, and if not for Mackenzie's arms and chest keeping her stable she might have slumped to the floor. Colby wanted the kiss to end and wanted it to go on forever. The decision was taken out of her hands when she heard the clack of heels and the sound of laughter made giddy by alcohol.

Mackenzie must have heard the voices because she wrenched her mouth away. She looked as if she wanted to say something. Colby stepped backward, shivering at the loss of Mackenzie's sexually charged body heat.

"Trust me?" Mackenzie pleaded.

Without thought, without hesitation, Colby nodded, and Mackenzie's arms were around her waist lifting her and carrying her into a shower stall. Colby heard the door push open just as Mackenzie set her down. Her breath left her chest in a soft puff as her back hit the cool tile seconds before Mackenzie's hand landed next to her head. Laughter rang out from two women discussing how badly someone had aged over the years. But for Colby, the voices faded as she stared into the most turbulent storm she had ever seen. Not quite true. She had seen this same typhoon of confusion in Mackenzie's face ten years earlier. Then, just like now, she hadn't known how to deal with it.

CHAPTER TWO

Roheibeth High School 1996

Colby was halfway to the lunchroom when she remembered she'd left her yearbook in the girls' locker room. She'd wanted to ask Beth Hartwell to sign it, but she had never gotten the nerve to make the request.

Female voices pitched abnormally high and male voices pitched artificially low traveled down the halls of Roheibeth High. Colby sighed as she pushed her way into the locker room. The line would be long by the time she got there, and she would get the stuff stuck to the bottom of the pan. This could actually be a good thing depending on what was on the menu for the day.

Colby hated lunchtime. She felt as if everyone was watching and noticing that she ate alone. Although she didn't consider them friends, when she hung out with anyone, it was other members of the computer club. Most of them brought their lunch so the whole hour could be used to play Dungeons and Dragons rather than losing the fifteen minutes it would take to stand in line. Colby would have preferred to avoid the lunchroom as well, but her mother consistently forgot to go to the grocery store, so there was never anything to pack for lunch. Breakfast was whatever Burger City had on special. Dinner was usually from the diner up the street. Colby loved the diner's fried chicken salads with ranch dressing. The forty-year-old guy who did the cooking usually added a little extra chicken to hers. The thought of the lecherous smile he gave her when he handed over her food made her stomach quail a little, but not as much as when she rounded the corner and saw Mackenzie Brandt sitting on a bench hunched over Colby's yearbook, her pencil moving rapidly.

"What are you doing? That's mine." The words tore from her lips seconds before the realization that she had made a drastic mistake.

The startled look on Mackenzie's face would have been funny if it had lasted long, but it didn't. It was soon replaced by an emotion Colby was familiar with—anger. Mackenzie slammed the yearbook closed, set it down on the bench, and stood with predatory deliberateness.

"Yours? How do I know it's yours?" she said. "That could be anyone's yearbook."

If it had been anyone but Mackenzie Brandt, Colby would have asked why she would sign a yearbook if she didn't know who it belonged to. But Colby hadn't been skipped up a grade for nothing. "My name is in the inside flap. Here, I'll show you." She walked closer and reached around Mackenzie, inadvertently brushing her leg with her hand. Mackenzie gasped and stepped back.

Colby backed away empty-handed. "Sorry," she said even though she had barely touched her. She had the bad habit of apologizing for things that weren't her fault, especially when she was nervous.

Mackenzie picked up the book and turned it over in her hands as if she had never seen it before. "If this is what you want, come and get it."

Colby was proud she only hesitated for a moment before reaching out and grasping the edge of the book. The plan was to take the yearbook—gently, of course—and run the hell out of there.

The smile on Mackenzie's face was the first tip things weren't going to be as easy as a snatch and dash, but she was determined to try anyway. Colby's face must have tipped Mackenzie off because she suddenly pulled the yearbook back and tucked it under her arm. "Wait, how do I know this is yours?"

Colby almost cried out in disappointment. Colby nodded toward the yearbook. "If you open the front cover, it should say 'this book belongs to Colby Dennis.' Oh, sorry. Uh, that's me. I have..." Colby started patting the pockets of her jeans. "I have my student ID."

"I know who you are."

"You do?"

Mackenzie nodded but didn't speak. *Why does she look so nervous?* Colby went on guard for one of Mackenzie's cronies to jump out from behind one of the lockers and beat the shit out of her. Not that Mackenzie had ever done much more than steal whatever romance novel she was reading, or bump her into a locker on the way to the lunch room, or ask to "borrow" a dollar they both knew she would never pay back, but there was a first time for everything. Colby started to back away.

"Where are you going? I thought you wanted this?"

"You can have it," Colby said, needing to put distance between herself and Mackenzie.

Like the flip of a switch, the angry expression Colby was used to was back. With two long strides, Mackenzie closed the gap between them. Before Colby could react, the front of her shirt was being crumpled in Mackenzie's fist and she was yanked close enough to smell spearmint on Mackenzie's breath. Colby waited for a blow, but it never came.

"I don't want your yearbook. I just want to ask you a question."

"Lunch is almost over. I can, uh, let you borrow a dollar if you're a little short." Colby tried to reach into her pocket for her lunch money. Giving Mackenzie a dollar would mean she wouldn't have enough for fries with her burger, but it was worth it if it meant she was saved the humiliation and pain of being pummeled.

To her relief, she heard the sound of laughter as someone came into the locker room. "I know. God, who does he think he is asking me out? Like I would ever go…"

Colby's breath was snatched from her as she was suddenly shoved into the shower area of the locker room. In the two years she had been at Roheibeth High, she had never seen anyone use the stalls for anything but getting dressed. Colby had never worked up a real sweat in gym class, but she did at least try to wash up the important bits in the bathroom. Most of the girls in her class simply got dressed and went to lunch.

Colby's back hit the wall, and her breath left in a little gasp. She didn't know what she had done, but Mackenzie had the strangest look on her face.

"Don't wear this shirt anymore," Mackenzie whispered.

"I…but why? My mother bought it for me."

"I don't give a shit who bought it for you. Don't wear it." Mackenzie's fist twisted tighter in the shirt.

"Okay, I won't." Colby grimaced as she thought about the lie she would have to tell her mother when asked why she only wore the shirt on the weekend. The shirt had been an expensive gift, one Colby knew her family could ill afford. Mackenzie seemed to be fixating on something, and when Colby looked down she noticed her breasts strained against the fabric of the shirt, her nipples painfully evident even beneath her bra. Heat crept up Colby's neck.

Mackenzie suddenly released her and stared down at the crumpled front of the shirt. "I'm sorry," she said softly. Colby opened her mouth out of habit to tell her it was okay. Only the words never came. This wasn't somebody who had just bumped into her in the halls. This was the person who made her heart thud every time she looked at her. Who made it just a little harder to get up and come to this hellhole every morning. And now she thought she could just say sorry and that would be the end of it.

Colby pressed her lips tightly together and looked down at the ground.

"Hey?" Mackenzie sounded entirely too close, and Colby's anger was doused as quickly as it had flared up. Whatever Mackenzie was smoking was bound to wear off, leaving Colby in danger of a serious ass kicking.

"I said I was sorry about the shirt, okay?" Mackenzie's hand came up, and Colby braced herself, eyes closed so she wouldn't see the punch coming. The punch never came, but a gentle pressure settled over her chest. Colby looked down, past the ragged nails and the surprisingly feminine hand settled on her chest.

She bites them. What could make Mackenzie Brandt nervous enough to bite her nails? The thought was so intriguing it was several moments before it dawned on Colby that Mackenzie's hand was moving across the front of the shirt. A back-and-forth motion just above her breast. Was she trying to smooth out the wrinkles she had caused, or calm Colby down? Whatever her reasoning, Colby's heart rate was slowing, the muscles in her back relaxed. She licked her lips and sighed and then straightened quickly when she realized she had almost let her guard down.

"You want people to look at you in this shirt, right?" Mackenzie asked as she methodically and ineffectually smoothed the wrinkles she had created. The question sounded thoughtful, as if she were trying to make sense of something.

"What? No…" Now Colby understood. *She's nuts, and no one even knows I'm in here with her.* "I don't want anyone to look at me." Mackenzie took a deep, shuddering breath and finally looked at Colby. She looked confused, even scared. Colby wondered why she had never noticed how perfectly shaped Mackenzie's lips were. Colby shook her head, wondering how she could be admiring the person about to kick her ass. Besides, who in their right mind admired the shape of lips? Maybe Mackenzie wasn't the crazy one after all.

"Do you have a boyfriend? Did you wear the shirt for him?"

"You know I don't." Incredulity crept into Colby's voice before she could stop it.

"You sure? That's not what I heard."

Relief flooded Colby's stomach, soothing the nervous squall as it dawned on her what this was all about. "What do you…you mean Eddie? He isn't my boyfriend, he…is he yours?" Eddie Fletcher had, on a dare, kissed her. Colby remembered trying to wrench her mouth away from breath that was a mix of Pall Mall cigarettes and watermelon Hubba Bubba bubble gum.

Mackenzie's expression went from shock to amusement. When her amusement grew into a full-fledged smile, Colby decided crazy or not, Mackenzie did have the most beautiful lips, and now that she could see them, great teeth. Colby forgot her fear and openly stared. Mackenzie flushed, and her long lashes swept down as if to keep her emotions from being exposed. Colby looked down too, inexplicably embarrassed for them both.

"Why did you let him kiss you, then?" Mackenzie asked.

Colby shook her head, confused by the question and Mackenzie's soft tone. "I didn't let him…I hated it. I pushed him off me."

"He told me you liked it. That you wanted him to."

"Yeah, like I really want to be kissed in front of everyone by that shit-for-brains," Colby said and then sobered quickly. It wasn't the first time her mouth had gotten her into trouble, but Mackenzie didn't appear to be angered by her lapse.

"Good, because he won't be doing it again. I told him if he did, he'd be walking funny for the rest of his life." Mackenzie studied Colby's face and then nodded as if it had told her something.

"How did you know what happened? You weren't there." Colby was even more confused now. *What? Is she my protector now? Great, she'll want all my lunch money instead of just half.*

"I heard him bragging to his friends about it. He said…he said you are a good kisser."

"He did?" Colby hadn't been expecting that.

"Yeah, he did. I didn't believe him, though. I told him he

wouldn't know a good kisser if he bought one." Her next sentence came out in a rush. "I thought I would give it a try. You know, just to see what all the hoopla was about." Mackenzie stared at Colby as if she expected her to say something. Colby managed to part her lips and wet them, but that was about the extent of her input.

Mackenzie suddenly bent her knees, and when she came up, their lips were pressed together. Perspiration broke out on Colby's constantly moist forehead, and her glasses slid down on her nose. Mackenzie's grip loosened on the front of Colby's shirt as the kiss deepened and everything else stood still. Colby felt something. *Oh God, is that her hand?* It grazed her breast through the silk shirt. Surely this was a test. Mackenzie would stop soon, laugh at her, and tell everyone what a perv she was, right? Colby put her hand up to Mackenzie's chest to push her away. She had expected Mackenzie to be hard, all muscle. She was, but she was soft too. Why couldn't she open her eyes? Warmth bloomed in her stomach and spread lower. This feeling wasn't foreign. She already knew how much pressure and just where to touch for maximum pleasure. Almost as if she'd heard her, Mackenzie eased her leg between Colby's and pressed into her. Colby turned away, her gasp muffled by Mackenzie's shoulder.

"Okay?" Mackenzie's question caressed her ear. For the second time in as many days, she was being forced into a kiss. Only this time, to her embarrassment, she liked it. Colby sagged in defeat and nodded. She couldn't look up for fear she would see Mackenzie laughing at her. Colby's thoughts went to a romance she had just read where the heroine waited with bated breath for the hero to kiss her. *This is what bated breath feels like.*

Mackenzie pressed her forehead against Colby's, seeming not to care it was moist with sweat. Colby's throat worked on a whimper that wasn't released until they were kissing again.

This time, Mackenzie's lips were tentative, almost as if she were giving Colby permission to send her away. When Mackenzie opened her mouth wider, Colby was forced to do the same. To her utter shock, Mackenzie slipped her tongue into Colby's mouth.

This had to be more than just teasing, didn't it? Colby shivered, her breathing quickening as the kiss grew more demanding. The air from Mackenzie's nose tickled Colby's top lip, and she started to fear she would faint if she didn't get some air soon. Mackenzie drew back.

"You're supposed to breath through your nose," she said, not unkindly, and Colby nodded her head like a lunatic.

Mackenzie searched Colby's face. She seemed to be waiting for some kind of response, and as was her habit, Colby obliged lamely. "What...what are you doing?" Her tongue felt like Mackenzie had lulled it to sleep.

"What do you think I'm doing?" Mackenzie punctuated the question with another heartrending kiss. "What does it feel like I'm doing?"

It felt like she had just kicked her in the stomach. Colby wanted to ask her why she was kissing her like that. Followed by why had she stopped. Colby didn't know what she was supposed to feel until the tears prickled the backs of her eyes. Her kiss-numbed lips parted as if to say "oh no" before the first tear dropped down her cheek.

"Why, why are you crying? I didn't..." Suddenly, Mackenzie's body was no longer pressing her into the wall, and she felt equal parts relief and disappointment. It took her a minute to figure out why Mackenzie was no longer standing in front of her.

Mrs. Graves, Colby's second-period gym teacher, had Mackenzie by her upper arm and was hustling her out of the shower stall. She was almost as tall as Mackenzie and twice as wide. "I've had it with you, Mackenzie Brandt," she said as she pushed Mackenzie in front of her. Colby hurried after them, trying to catch her breath enough to tell Mrs. Graves she was making a mistake.

"Colby? Colby, tell her I wasn't hurting you. Mrs. Grave, wait, damn it." Mackenzie tried to brace herself in the door; she was looking at Colby, her expression pleading.

"Mrs. Graves, wait," Colby croaked out. "You don't

understand…" *What was she supposed to say? That she had enjoyed being kissed by Mackenzie Brandt? That she had wanted what was happening? How could she tell Mrs. Graves that?* Colby covered her mouth just as Mackenzie managed to make eye contact with her over Mrs. Graves's broad shoulder. *How could she tell anyone that?*

Mackenzie had been staring at her for what seemed like years; her eyes were pleading just like they had been in the shower stall. *What does she want from me?* Mrs. Graves forcefully pried Mackenzie's fingers from the doorjamb. A twisting smile appeared on Mackenzie's face. "It's been fun, Colby." Mackenzie's voice had taken on a gruff edge that always made Colby cringe. Colby followed them, still unable to say anything. Three times Mackenzie was able to get Mrs. Graves to slow down enough so she could glance back, and each time she did, her expression grew distant when Colby didn't say anything. Mrs. Graves pulled the heavy door to the office open and pushed Mackenzie into the room. "Go to class, Colby. I'll take care of this."

Colby wanted the door to slam shut so she could finally be released from whatever spell Mackenzie Brandt had cast over her. But it didn't. She watched as the door quietly clicked closed. And as if in a dream, Colby simply turned around and did as she was told. She went to class.

CHAPTER THREE

Roheibeth High School Class of 1996 Reunion

"Don't," Colby said, but her words were muffled by Mackenzie's sweet lips. What was she trying to say? Don't what? Don't kiss me? Don't make me want you? Maybe Mackenzie would have taken the order more seriously if Colby weren't caressing the back of her neck, encouraging her to increase the pressure.

Like ten years before. Mackenzie had her pinned firmly to the shower wall, but the tentative explorations of teenagers had long been forgotten. Mackenzie was a good kisser. *That's right. She is. Her husband is a lucky man.*

The thought was a bucket of cold water over embers. Colby turned her head away, blinking back frustrated tears. The only sound was their harsh breathing rebounding off the tile walls. "I've dreamt of doing that," Mackenzie said.

Colby's anger flared, hot licks fanned by the realization that she had dreamt of it too. She grabbed the back of Mackenzie's head and kissed her hard in an effort to wash away the fantasy feel of the moment. This wasn't about being sweet. This was about pleasure and fucking. About getting even and letting go of past baggage. Wasn't it?

Colby cupped the sides of Mackenzie's face and leaned back so she could look at her.

"You still want to apologize to me?" Colby asked softly.

Mackenzie licked her lips and nodded, managing to look both aroused and innocent at the same time. How could she have ever thought her menacing?

"I can't remember the last time I had sex. Let alone an orgasm." The startled look on Mackenzie's face made Colby smile. "What's the matter? You need to be the aggressor?"

"No, I...I'm just..."

"Never mind. This was probably a mistake." *What the hell was she asking her to do anyway?*

"It wasn't a mistake. Are you staying in a hotel?"

Colby's smile fell. She had figured she would push until Mackenzie backed down. Then she would walk away. Payback— short and sweet. She hadn't figured on Mackenzie taking her up on her offer. Colby started as she realized Mackenzie was still waiting for an answer. "Yes. But I think you should apologize here. Right now. With that beautiful mouth of yours."

Why in the hell had she said that? It wasn't like her. None of this was. Colby shivered, hating the way her body responded by instantly dampening her panties. Her clit became uncomfortably tight, and she shifted her stance. Mackenzie looked as if she were about to initiate another reason-dashing kiss, but Colby put her hand up to stop her. "Not like that." She kept her gaze direct until she was sure Mackenzie understood what she was implying. Colby's heart was slamming around her rib cage like a bird trying to escape its confines. She fully expected Mackenzie to turn around and walk out of the locker room calling her all kinds of bitches.

Instead, she pulled Colby into a tight hug that surprised Colby so much she returned it. Mackenzie turned her head slightly so her mouth was near Colby's ear stirring up memories of paperback romances read in secret on weekends that should have been spent with friends.

"I know what you're doing," Mackenzie said. "Promise me you'll let me talk to you after?"

After? After what? Stop this, Colby. Tell her what you're doing. Tell her why you're here. A flash of pride distracted Colby as Mackenzie's hands crept beneath her shirt and lingered on the ripples of her abs. She wondered if Mackenzie was comparing her body to how she had been ten years before. That was crazy. That kiss had been different, meant to humiliate and embarrass her. At least, that's the conclusion Colby had come to after days of replaying that moment over and over in her head. She had determined that the need and arousal she had sensed in Mackenzie had all been created by the overactive imagination of a teenager just beginning to suspect she was a lesbian.

Colby was yanked back to the present when Mackenzie suddenly dropped to her knees and pushed Colby's dress up around her hips. *It's time to stop. Things have gone too far.* But knowing what Mackenzie was willing to do, what she *wanted* desperately to do, made it hard for Colby to think clearly. Finally, Colby grabbed Mackenzie's wrists and pulled her back to her feet. Before she could utter the words neither of them wanted to hear, Mackenzie stopped her with a finger to her lips.

"Don't say anything, Colby. Let me do this for you." Colby's groan of protest died in her throat when Mackenzie touched the soaked crotch of her panties. An instant later, Mackenzie's warm fingers had pushed the flimsy cloth aside, parted her lips, and began stroking the shaft of her clitoris too gently for satisfaction. Colby had to grit her teeth hard to keep from begging for more. She dropped her forehead on Mackenzie's shoulder, grateful for the height difference that allowed her to hide the fact she was biting the hell out of her bottom lip to keep from crying out. Mackenzie entered her with no hesitation and quickly found the perfect rhythm. Her hand steady, her fingers powerful but gentle.

Any second now I'm going to scream so loud my whole high school class is going to know I'm getting the daylights fucked out of me. Bet they'd remember me after that. The thought was just the sobering effect she needed. Mackenzie straightened, her face was intense as she searched Colby's. Mackenzie was obviously as uncomfortably aroused as she was. *Damn, was she always this intense? When did she become so damn sexy?*

"Wait." Colby should have felt pleasure when she saw disappointment cross Mackenzie's face, but it was hard to think like that while Mackenzie's fingers, and the pleasure they had been giving her, were slipping away.

Colby's clit throbbed painfully as if to say "What did you do that for, stupid bitch?" The wall and Mackenzie's torso were the only things keeping her upright. "Give me a little space. I'm not going anywhere. I promise." Mackenzie reluctantly stepped back so their bodies were no longer touching. Colby kept eye contact with Mackenzie while she reached beneath her dress and pushed her panties down and off. Mackenzie took Colby's panties from her and put them in her pants pocket.

"My, how you've progressed. Panties instead of lunch money and romance novels?"

Mackenzie raised an eyebrow. "I would have been happy to take your panties back then too." Any response Colby would have made was forgotten when Mackenzie stepped between her legs, hiked her dress up above her hips, and pressed the seam of her trousers against Colby's exposed vagina.

Colby's gasp was loud and aroused. There was no hiding it now. Mackenzie devoured her mouth, and Colby dropped all pretense and kissed her back while grinding her hips with escalating force. There was no longer any reason to pretend. Mackenzie already knew how aroused she was since she had been inside her. Colby let another moan escape and pushed the thought away. If she expected to last longer than a few more moments, she had to keep her mind in the here and now.

Mackenzie kneeled between Colby's legs, leaving her open and exposed. Anticipation, coupled with fear, left her feeling anchorless. Colby blushed as Mackenzie stared at her sex for a long moment.

"I knew you would be this beautiful," Mackenzie said before

she leaned in and kissed Colby's labia, a soft, sweet, soulful kiss that made Colby whimper. Colby was reminded of how small she had felt ten years earlier when Mackenzie had towered over her in this very same locker room. She still felt that way, only now she felt cherished too. Mackenzie parted her with her tongue and lavished so much attention on Colby's clitoris that Colby was afraid she wouldn't be able to stand up. Colby rested her hand on the top of Mackenzie's head, not steering, not encouraging, just wanting Mackenzie to remember she was there.

A low bump came from somewhere in the locker room, and she stiffened. "Did you see how fat she's gotten? Good Lord, you'd think the woman would have stopped at the first four." Either Mackenzie was concentrating too hard on what she was doing or she didn't care, because her lips and tongue never faltered. Colby tightened her grip on Mackenzie's hair but couldn't bring herself to push her away.

"Yeah, I know. There is no way I would have let myself go like that. Her husband's kind of cute, though. Did you see him?" The sound of laughter was drowned out by toilets flushing. Colby involuntarily thrust her hips out so Mackenzie could have greater access to her, and Mackenzie took advantage, cupping her hips as she sank her tongue deep into Colby's opening. Colby felt her eyes roll back. She was too close. She needed to make Mackenzie stop before she—

"She was such a slut in high school. Do you really think all those kids are his?"

Mackenzie moved so quickly Colby had no time to think. Mackenzie used her considerable strength to seat Colby on her shoulders. Colby arched her back, shoulders braced against the tiled walls to give Mackenzie full access. Colby gritted her teeth and dug both hands into Mackenzie's hair. It was simultaneously too much and everything she had ever wanted.

The sounds they were making seemed to be amplified. She expected to hear one of the two voices suddenly say, "Did you hear that?" She didn't think she could stop if they did. Fuck them. She knew she couldn't, and if Mackenzie tried to, she would clamp down on her so hard she'd probably do damage. Mackenzie seemed intent on drowning in Colby.

Colby reached down and made a weak attempt at pushing Mackenzie's head back, but Mackenzie shook her head, sending a wave of pleasure shooting through her. Colby went limp; there was nothing she could do. Her attempt at humiliating Mackenzie had backfired.

"All right, let's get back out there before all the single men are taken…" The door thumped closed, and Mackenzie thrust her tongue deep inside Colby and pulled out, running her tongue along the shaft of her clitoris before sinking deeply once more. Colby gasped, thrusting her hips out for more, and Mackenzie gave until Colby couldn't think past the pleasure she was receiving. Colby was still shivering when Mackenzie gently lowered first her right foot and then her left and smoothed her skirt down over her hips. Mackenzie pulled Colby's panties from her pocket and slowly wiped her mouth with them. Colby shuddered from both residual orgasm and the unspoken promise. Mackenzie was telling her, in no uncertain terms, there was more where that came from.

"Now can we talk?" Mackenzie asked.

Mackenzie's words and the cold feeling in Colby's chest brought back the seriousness of what she had done. "No, I…I can't. I have to go. I'm sorry," Colby said and walked out of the shower and toward the exit.

"Colby? What the hell?"

Colby turned around and looked back at Mackenzie. She expected to see anger—hell, *she* would have been angry—but what she saw was hurt. Plain and simple. No pretense, just someone who had been hurt. "I'm sorry. I can't do this. Not with you." Colby turned and walked out of the locker room.

❖

Colby waited in the line at the punch bowl to get her keys. There was a lot of laughing and jostling going on that was trying her patience. Some people were having a hard time proving they were capable of driving home and were being forced to take a cab. Colby felt she hadn't had enough to drink to deal with possibly seeing Mackenzie. What the hell had just happened? She had gone from wanting to exorcise old demons, to wanting revenge, to just…wanting. The strange part was it hadn't felt all that different from what she'd felt in high school. Had she always felt that strange burst of adrenaline when she caught sight of Mackenzie? Colby's breath caught when she saw Mackenzie walk out of the locker room.

"Do you have your claim check?" Colby turned back to the woman who was, according to her name tag, Paul Zanziger's wife—whoever the hell he was. "Um, no, I must have lost it." *Yeah, while I was wallowing around in a public bathroom with a woman I haven't seen in years.* "Never mind. I think I'll take a cab."

Paul Zanziger's wife looked at her rumpled dress and hair and nodded sternly. "That's probably a good idea. Someone poured way too much rum in the punch."

"Um, yeah." Colby turned away and ran right into Mackenzie just as Toni Braxton's "Unbreak My Heart" blared over the loud speakers. Some guy wearing way too much Drakkar cologne pushed past. Colby felt drunk even though she had only had one sip of the punch. Mackenzie's eyes were dark and hard to read, but the purposely blank look on her face wasn't. Either someone had turned up Toni Braxton or the heat in the room was getting to her, because Colby swayed. An alarmed look flared across Mackenzie's face, and she reached out to steady her.

"No," Colby said loudly and stepped back. "I'm fine, just tired. Traffic was bad. It was a long drive up from Portland. I'm going to head back to my hotel."

Mackenzie stepped to the side, and Colby rushed past her. After someone else's wife handed Colby her coat, she escaped into the crisp night air and filled her lungs in the hope of clearing her head.

"They didn't plan this very well." A woman Colby vaguely recognized was complaining to two other people. "They should have had cabs waiting out here if they were going to force us to take them." Colby joined the three other "drunks" waiting for the cab.

A tall man with a prominent potbelly nodded his agreement. Colby recognized him as a former popular basketball player. Ten years ago he had been reed thin, and according to the girls' bathroom gossip, "So damn fine!" Colby sighed. At this rate, she would be better off waiting for Mackenzie to leave so she could find her claim ticket and retrieve her car keys. Not that Paul Zanziger's wife would believe her if she now claimed to be sober enough to drive.

The door to the gym swung open, and Mackenzie walked out. She seemed as surprised to see Colby as Colby was to see her.

She looks sad. The pang of guilt made Colby angry. After all the cruel things the woman had done to her, why should she care if she made her sad? Still, she couldn't help but sneak peeks at Mackenzie.

"Finally, here's one. If any of you are going to the hotel, we can share. Otherwise, you might have a long wait." The woman—Colby thought her name started with a *K*; Kristal or Kristie or something like that—laughed, and Colby seriously considered waiting on the next cab when she smelled the rum on the woman's breath. One by one, all of them said they were going to the hotel. Without a word, the former basketball player got in the front seat and strapped his seat belt on.

"Well," Colby said, "I guess that leaves the backseat for the rest of us."

"How about you? You headed to the hotel?" the driver called out to Mackenzie.

"Close, but I'll wait for the next one."

"Might be a while," the driver said. "Lots of business at the airport tonight for some reason. You might as well hop in with these guys. Otherwise, you'll just have to wait for me to come back." Colby felt the hairs on the back of her neck stand up as Mackenzie approached. They were both steadfastly ignoring each other. The woman with the rum breath and her two male companions had already entered the cab. The back door was open, and there was only space for one more body. The driver looked at his clock. "No cops out around here tonight. If someone is willing to let you sit on their lap…"

"No, thanks. I'll just wait." The cabby shrugged and got into the driver's seat. Colby was about to get into the car when she looked around the dark parking lot and shivered. Mackenzie had never been a slouch, and from the looks of her, she had continued to work out over the years. She could no doubt take care of herself, but Colby didn't like the idea of leaving her standing in a deserted parking lot waiting for a cab.

"You can sit on my lap if you want," Colby offered and then could have kicked herself. First she'd ran out on the woman after asking her to go down on her, and now she was asking her to sit on her lap.

"Thanks for the offer," Mackenzie said softly, "but my legs are too long, and I'm a lot heavier than I look."

"Come on. It's getting cold." Colby ducked to glare at Kristal, but she had already leaned her head back, as had the guy sitting next to her. The guy in the front seat had fallen asleep. His head lolled forward, and a slow, buzzing snore was emanating from his nose. The cabby seemed content to let the meter run.

Colby got in the car and looked back at Mackenzie. "Would you come on? Do I look like I can't handle your weight? You're going to freeze to death out there." Mackenzie reluctantly approached the door, and Colby scooted back in the seat, giving Mackenzie as much leg room as she could. Mackenzie looked as if she wanted to continue to protest but instead got into the car, settling gingerly on Colby's lap and pulling the door shut behind her. The cab eased out of the parking lot and bumped gently onto the road. Colby was thinking Mackenzie was nowhere near as heavy as she'd claimed, until she noticed the white-knuckled grip Mackenzie had on the seat in front of her.

"Stop that," Colby said, irritated for some reason. "I'm not going to bite you." Her voice was a hiss she hoped only Mackenzie heard. "Lean back."

Mackenzie looked to the right to make sure the two dark figures next to them were really as asleep as they appeared, and then she leaned back to speak to Colby. "You should have let me wait for the next cab. I know this is probably uncomfortable for you."

God, why is she being so damn nice about this?

Mackenzie continued to hold herself up slightly until Colby wrapped her arms around her waist and forcibly pulled her back. Mackenzie's tummy constricted beneath her hands, and Colby spread her fingers wide, mesmerized by the feel of silken skin. Mackenzie had obviously spent a lot of time keeping her body in shape. If anything, it was better than when they were in high school. Not that it hadn't been great in high school. Colby focused on the last thought. Had she noticed Mackenzie's body in high school? How could she? Mackenzie wore baggy jeans and a sweatshirt ninety-nine percent of the time. Yet she had noticed, hadn't she?

Mackenzie's stomach had not relaxed beneath her hands, and Colby began to rub it absentmindedly as she mulled over the idea. All her memories of Mackenzie were unpleasant, weren't they? Well, the last time they had seen each other before tonight hadn't been…unpleasant. Not really. Not at all.

"Relax," she tried to whisper in Mackenzie's ear but only reached her shoulder. Mackenzie didn't release the death grip on the seat in front of her despite Colby having forced her to lean back. Colby shifted so that Mackenzie's weight was more evenly distributed. Mackenzie hadn't lied. She was much heavier than she looked, but Colby liked the feel of it. Her gentle rubs didn't seem to be working, so she eased Mackenzie's shirt out of her pants and rubbed her bare stomach. Mackenzie inhaled, and Colby spent a few blissful moments enjoying the rock-hard plains of Mackenzie's muscles. Colby went to the gym a minimum of four times a week, forty-five minutes to an hour a day, and yet Mackenzie had to have lived in the gym. Colby looked over at the other passengers in the cab and at the driver who was busy adjusting something on his meter and nodding to the beat of some song only he was hearing.

Colby whispered into Mackenzie's shoulder. "You feel good." Mackenzie shuddered and finally seemed to relax. "Aren't you more comfortable now?" Mackenzie nodded but didn't say anything.

Colby's fingers dipped just below Mackenzie's waistband, and Mackenzie inhaled just loud enough to be heard. Colby plucked at Mackenzie's pants buttons, more to see what her reaction would be than any real intention to unfasten them. But when Mackenzie lifted her hips slightly to give her better access, Colby felt her arousal flare, and she lifted her own hips in response.

Mackenzie's buttons came loose easily, and Colby wasted no time sinking beneath her damp underwear to slip one finger between heated folds. Mackenzie jumped, and had Colby not moved her head to the side, she might have been injured when Mackenzie's head suddenly came back. Her index finger stroked the shaft of Mackenzie's clitoris, and Colby realized how painfully turned on Mackenzie was. She looked at the sleeping figures of her companions and up at the cab driver to make sure he wasn't sneaking furtive looks in his rearview mirror. With a beckoning motion, she both pulled Mackenzie back and entered her. She felt Mackenzie's thighs tremble and thought she heard her moan. Mackenzie leaned her head back and rested it on Colby's shoulder. Colby whispered in her ear, "I am so sorry for not taking care of this earlier. Now let go of the seat."

Mackenzie obediently released the headrest, and the front seat passenger's head bobbed. "Good, now open your legs as wide as you can."

In the crowded backseat, Mackenzie was only able to move a few inches, but it was enough. Colby straightened her own body, bringing Mackenzie into a more upright position that brought her deeper inside Mackenzie's heat. Mackenzie was breathing hard now, and Colby kept an eye on the cab driver to make sure he wasn't paying attention. She was wrong for doing this here, but she couldn't help it. Not with Mackenzie. There was something so painfully attractive about her.

Mackenzie's hands went to the car seat, and again Colby told her to let go. Mackenzie immediately released the seat, and her hands went to Colby's wrist to help her go deeper. "Lean back now," Colby ordered. "I'm going to make you come. Are you ready?" When Mackenzie nodded, Colby lifted her hips, pressing down with her thighs, temporarily straightening Mackenzie's body and thrusting hard inside her. She pressed her two fingers deep inside Mackenzie while pressing down hard with her thumb on Mackenzie's clitoris. Mackenzie's body stiffened, and Colby quickened her pace.

If their two companions weren't so intoxicated, they would have been awakened by the motion, but neither had moved since they had gotten into the car. Colby checked the mirror again to make sure the driver wasn't looking. Mackenzie's thighs clamped hard on her hand, and Colby half expected her to shout. But the hands gripping her wrists went to Mackenzie's mouth, and to Colby's mild disappointment, Mackenzie held the scream in while her hips jumped wildly beneath Colby's hand.

Any worry Mackenzie had about crushing Colby must have disappeared because all her weight collapsed on Colby. Colby slowly zipped and buttoned Mackenzie's trousers. Tucking the shirt was next to impossible, but she doubted anyone would notice.

It took five minutes for the cab to pull into the circular driveway of the hotel, and it took Mackenzie the whole time to regain her breathing.

"All right, folks, we're here." The cabby's voice seemed to clash with the quiet of the cab, and with a rum-infused snort and a jump, the woman next to them sat up. Mackenzie had the door open and was clamoring out on unsteady feet.

The other three passengers paid their share of the cab ride while Colby studied Mackenzie. "Do you want to come up?"

Mackenzie looked at her for a long moment, seemed to consider it, and then shook her head. "I'm sorry, I can't."

"Someone waiting for you at home?" Colby pushed down the flash of anger. Why did she even bother asking a question she knew the answer to? "Never mind. It doesn't matter. I'm leaving tomorrow, so…"

Mackenzie looked startled. "Tomorrow? Can I see you before you go?"

"I…no. I have several client meetings Monday that I need to prepare for."

"Oh, okay." Her face showed the disappointment that her words did not. Again, Mackenzie's willingness to show her emotions confused Colby. She had not been so open when they were in high school. What had changed her so drastically?

"I could give you a call sometime. Maybe we could—"

Colby's question was interrupted by Kristal calling out a companionable, "Bye, you two."

Colby waved and turned back to Mackenzie. "Maybe we could meet somewhere and have lunch." Colby thought her offer sounded lame after what they had just done, but Mackenzie was already nodding.

"I'd like that. I'd still like to explain about high school."

Colby suddenly remembered what she was doing and who she was doing it with. She didn't need to remind herself how much of a mistake she'd just made by having sex with Mackenzie, but why was she making plans with her? Sex was one thing, but conversation? What was the point in that?

"We should get going, ladies," the driver interrupted, and Colby hastily removed a bill from the tiny pocket hidden in the seam of her dress. "Wait for her. She says she lives close."

Colby clumsily wrapped her arms around Mackenzie's waist. "Good-bye, Mackenzie," she said, and Mackenzie returned the hug.

"Call me, okay?"

Colby nodded but didn't meet Mackenzie's eyes, and walked into the hotel. What the hell was she doing?

CHAPTER FOUR

Dennis Security, Inc., Portland, Oregon

Colby sat looking at the picture for a few moments before closing the file and picking up her now cooled mug of coffee. She hadn't had such a bad lapse in judgment in a very long time. It wasn't as if she was some sex-starved teenager, for God's sake. She would be thirty in the blink of an eye and was quite content with going months without sex. So why had she been unable to pass up the opportunity this time? And why would she suddenly lose her senses with Mackenzie Brandt, of all people?

Colby placed her hands on her cheeks to cool them. Every time she thought of her, of what they had done, her body flushed. She'd been replaying the sensation and feel of Mackenzie since she had returned to Portland three days ago. Although they hadn't exchanged numbers, Mackenzie seemed to know Colby would have no trouble finding her. Colby sighed. Mackenzie was right. Normally it was as easy as turning on a computer screen for Colby to get even an unlisted phone number. In Mackenzie's case, it had been easier than that.

The intercom on her desk buzzed. Colby hit the button and forced the weariness from her tone. "Send them in, Asia," she said without waiting for her assistant to announce her guests.

Colby stood and was halfway around the desk when Arnult

and Barb Copeland swept into the room like two movie icons walking a red carpet lined with photographers.

What was it about this elderly, impeccably dressed, gray-haired couple that set Colby's teeth on edge?

The Copelands seated themselves without being invited, and Colby leaned out the door and looked Asia pointedly in the eye. "I will be with the Copelands for a while. Please hold all my calls." Asia nodded her understanding. She always held her calls during meetings with clients. Colby only reminded her to do it when she wanted her to interrupt if the meeting went on too long. Thirty minutes was long enough to brush off a problem client. In the case of the Copelands, she was hoping it would be less. Her curiosity was what kept her from having this conversation over the phone.

Colby had barely shut the door before Arnult Copeland began to speak.

"Ms. Dennis, thank you for seeing us. Am I to assume you will be seeing to our situation personally?"

Now she knew what rubbed her the wrong way about these two. It was the way they assumed their age and financial status afforded them special provisions.

"I sensed when we first spoke that you didn't think our situation was *worthy* of your time."

Arnult's condescending tone didn't help matters either. But he was correct; she hadn't thought an infidelity case was worthy of Dennis Security's time until she'd opened the file they had left with her. All the armor she had clothed herself with over the past ten years had been stripped from her in seconds.

"All cases are worthy of my time, Mr. Copeland. But I can't handle them all personally anymore. That's why I have associates. Surely you understand?" Colby tried to appeal to his business side, but when the couple looked uncomfortably at each other and then back at her, she realized there was more to this than they were telling her.

Barb Copeland spoke first. "Surely *you* understand the

delicate nature of our situation after reading the file we left for you."

Colby ran her thumb over her lips in frustration. She hadn't read the entire file. She hadn't gotten past the first picture and subject bio. She had just reacted.

Arnult Copeland took the baton from his wife and decided to run with it. "Our son Nickolas has hopes of running for public office some day. If any of this gets out, it could be devastating. You were recommended highly by an old friend of mine, Edward Mathews."

Colby nodded, grateful Arnult had finally shown his hand. She'd been wondering why the Copelands had sought her out for such a seemingly mundane task. Edward had probably told his "old buddy" exactly how much money his law firm sent her way annually. No, Arnult wasn't just name-dropping, he was explaining to her in the nicest terms exactly why she needed to handle his situation personally.

Under other circumstances Colby might have laughed. The loss of Edward Mathews as a client, if it came to that, would be noticeable but not cataclysmic to her business. Colby had never been one to put all her eggs in one basket. Consequently, money had ceased to be a deciding factor in the cases she took on. No, the reason the Copelands were in front of her now was for one reason and one reason only. Their daughter-in-law was Mackenzie Brandt.

Colby steepled her fingers in front of her and looked first at Mr. Copeland and then at Mrs. Copeland. "What will you do with the proof if I'm able to provide it?"

Mrs. Copeland's eyes grew wide. "Nothing, of course. We don't want the information out any more than she does. This is simply an insurance policy we want to take out for our son."

"How is proving your son's wife is a lesbian an insurance policy?" The confident look faded from Arnult's face, and Barb Copeland blanched. Colby felt a mean little thrill of pleasure and not one shred of guilt.

"She's planning to file for divorce."

"Mackenzie is filing for divorce?" Colby spoke without thinking. She hadn't expected that. Nor did she expect the feeling of lightness that blossomed over her. It was the thought that followed that scared her. *Maybe it didn't have to be a one-nighter, after all.* "Does your son know she's divorcing him?"

"Yes. They haven't come to us about it yet, but I suspect it will happen any day now."

Colby felt as if all the air had left her lungs. "Then why do you care if she's seeing someone else? Or is it just because the someone else is a woman?"

"We believe there have been many someone elses. The truth of the matter is, we don't want to see our son caught unawares by other matters. We are positive he has no idea she's been unfaithful to this extent."

Bet you don't know how good at it she is. Colby pushed the thought away.

"He's a kind man, Ms. Dennis. He will continue to have a relationship with her unless we prove she's unworthy of his attention. He isn't thinking of his future. But we are."

"His future?" Colby knew she should just tell them the truth. Well, part of it, anyway. She didn't feel she could take the case since she had gone to school with their daughter-in-law. Of course she couldn't mention the sex thing, or that she had been unable to get the woman out of her mind afterward. Besides, if she told them that, they would no doubt walk out of her office and find someone else. *Wait. Isn't that the idea?*

"Our family has a long history of public service," Barb Copeland explained proudly. "Divorce is frowned upon in our circle." *Roheibeth has circles?* Colby was having a hard time keeping a straight face.

"But if we can prove she's had numerous affairs—with *other women.* Well, no one will hold Nick responsible for the divorce. It might even help him in the long run. Especially if he finds someone more appropriate."

"I see," Colby said, and she did. This was all about status in the community. Something neither she nor her parents had ever had or cared about. "How did you find out?"

"Our son had the good sense to call our family attorney to get a referral for a divorce attorney. Our lawyer thought it prudent to alert us."

"It might have been prudent, but I'm not sure how ethical it was for him to tell you about your son's business. But I was asking how you found out your daughter-in-law was a lesbian."

Barb's mouth turned down. She cleared her throat and pulled a kerchief from her purse as if she were about to burst into tears. "She's been seen, and it wasn't the first time. She is promiscuous, and we would like nothing better than to have our son distance himself from her."

Fuck! If a strong wind had meandered up the stairwell to the ninth floor of her office building, it could have easily knocked Colby over. *Promiscuous?* What the fuck had she been thinking having unprotected sex with a stranger? That was just it. She hadn't been thinking. She had been feeling. She had been suckered. Suckered by a pro, and this time it cost her more than a dollar. She should have known better. She should have known no one changed that much.

Of course Mackenzie was different. It should have been no surprise to her that high school bullies grew up and turned into manipulative, money-grubbing sluts who got their kicks out of tricking dim-witted women into bed—or in her case, locker rooms. What didn't make sense was if Colby was one of many conquests, why had Mackenzie looked so thunderstruck when Colby had walked away from her?

Anger threatened, but then she calmed herself. What was there to be angry about? She had enjoyed being with Mackenzie. Yet it was more than just anger that made her want to push the Copelands out of her office so she could be alone.

As much as she would have loved to see Mackenzie's face when she realized Colby was working for her in-laws, she was too close to this situation to be objective. In fact, any objectivity was out the window when she'd opened the file and seen the photo of Mackenzie Brandt. It didn't matter really, did it? No matter if she turned this man down or not, he would find someone else to get his information. That person would have sense enough not to get personally involved. Mackenzie would get what was coming to her, no matter what. She didn't need to be involved. All she had to do was keep her mouth shut and stay out of it.

"Ms. Dennis?" Arnult Copeland held up his checkbook as if it were the answer to whatever was bothering Colby.

Colby stared at the checkbook. As soon as she gave him a definitive no he would look for someone else. Someone else would get the chance to take the wind out of Mackenzie's sails, and that someone wouldn't have the grudge she did.

"All right, I'll handle your situation," Colby said, and her heart slid to the soles of her feet where it would, she guessed, join her brain and common sense.

"Personally?" Arnult asked, though his tone implied he knew the answer.

"Yes, personally." *It would be my pleasure.*

"Good. Glad to hear it." Arnult stood.

"At twice my usual retainer, seeing as this is a delicate situation that can only be handled by me. You can make the check out to Dennis Security, thank you."

Arnult sat back down and nodded as if it were his idea to pay her the ungodly sum. He wordlessly filled out the check, ripped it from the book, and handed it to her with a flourish. Colby stood, shook both their hands, and ushered them from her office. She was glaring down at the check when Asia returned. "I thought you were going to refer that case out."

"Good news travels fast. Do me a favor and run a background on Mackenzie Brandt—Copeland."

"Will do. And for the record, no one had to tell me. That guy looked like he had just swallowed up a small mom-and-pop and turned it into a chain store. So what made you change your mind?"

Colby cleared her throat. "He's an old friend of Edward's." Asia's mouth formed into an *O* as if that explained it all. Her reaction bugged the shit out of Colby. What was she thinking, getting involved in this? She should have shown Arnult and Barb the door—hell, she never should have even gone to the reunion. She certainly shouldn't have asked Barb and Arnult to meet with her a second time. But when she had opened the file and seen the picture of Mackenzie, she had felt trapped. Her going to the reunion had been a way to prove to herself that her reaction had been a fantasy, that meeting her, seeing her in person would cure her of whatever ailment had latched on to her common senses. Damn it, she was losing it.

"Okay, so I get why Dennis Security had to take the case, but why are you handling it? Anyone could do this. You haven't done this kind of stuff in...well, not since I've been here."

"I grew up in their hometown, went to school with their daughter-in-law." She left out the part about how their daughter-in-law had made her life hell. What would be the point of pouring more ink in pitch black waters?

"So it's personal?"

"Yeah, something like that."

"I guess we should see about clearing your calendar, then." Asia picked up a notepad and the retainer check from Colby's desk.

"Um, I better hang on to that. I made him pay twice the amount because he annoyed me, but I'd rather not have to deal with the paperwork of giving the guy a refund if this is a flip trip."

"You think it'll be that fast?"

Colby knew her smile was grim. "If she's as promiscuous as the Copelands seem to think, a day, maybe two."

CHAPTER FIVE

Fit Life Fitness Center, Roheibeth, Oregon

As a personal trainer, Mackenzie felt it was important for her to give new clients one hundred percent of her attention. It wasn't that she found everything they said riveting—she usually got all the information she needed in the first few seconds of conversation—it was more that she had learned clients tended to hide things once they knew her. It was as if they believed that if they confessed that they couldn't care less about fitness levels and just wanted to look good, it would disappoint her. The reason she couldn't keep her mind on her work was the same one that had been riding her consciousness for the last week: She hadn't heard from Colby Dennis. Deep down, she hadn't really expected to, and she was both upset she'd had sex with Colby and tormented by the memory of how good she had felt while doing it.

The two-minute session on the treadmill ended, and her potential new client seemed winded but not at all exhausted. It seemed odd to Mackenzie since she had checked the box stipulating she hadn't worked out continuously in years. Mackenzie studied her body, noting the sports bra and tight-fitting shorts. The shoes she wore were actually running shoes, not some "athletic shoe" that would tear up within months of starting to train.

"Great workout," Mackenzie told her and then tossed her a

fresh towel as she stepped gracefully off the treadmill. Mackenzie wouldn't have normally put a new client through such a rigorous workout, but she had sensed this woman could handle it. Sure enough, she had wordlessly nodded when Mackenzie told her she was going to have her run for two minutes on an incline all-out.

Her new client—Mackenzie temporarily blanked on her name and then came up with Jessie—smiled and wiped her forehead, though there was little if any sweat there.

Jessie smiled at her. "Wow, I feel like I'm going to puke." Mackenzie frowned at her. She didn't look like she was going to puke. In fact, she looked to be in great physical shape. Mackenzie shifted from one foot to the other and felt a small tingle of awareness when Jessie boldly looked at her body, her smile softening around the edges in what Mackenzie realized was an invitation.

"Do you remember where the showers are?" Mackenzie had never felt so off-kilter. She'd had her fair share of men come on to her. Women, on the other hand, were another story, and the one standing in front of her was attractive. But even if Mackenzie hadn't had a policy against dating clients, she wouldn't take this woman up on the invitation. Not so soon after the mess with Colby. Besides, there was something off-putting about Jessie. Mackenzie couldn't help but feel she was trying too hard.

"Yeah, I remember where they are. How about you? You said I was your last client. Care to join me?"

Mackenzie felt her face go hot. They had progressed from subtle to blatant come-ons rather fast. Did things like this happen? Not according to her good friend Palmer. Palmer claimed if Mackenzie ever wanted to get laid on a regular basis, she would have to be the one doing the pursuing because she fell too neatly in between the labels lesbians like to slap on each other. Mackenzie still hadn't been able to muster up the courage to tell Palmer what happened with Colby. Palmer wouldn't understand she hadn't been looking for sex.

Palmer had asked, but Mackenzie had only been able to

admit that Colby and she still had issues. She had hoped they would be able to work them out, but she had a feeling the sex had kiboshed that plan entirely. She still got aroused thinking about it, but she hoped she would do things differently if she had another chance.

"I meant in the adjoining shower, and I'm starving. I was hoping you'd join me for dinner."

Mackenzie was saved from having to answer by a loud, cheery hello. Nick walked in wearing a smile that would have turned most straight women's hearts into a warm puddle. Mackenzie sighed.

"Sorry, I'm a little late," he said.

"Um, Jessie, this is my...husband." She turned to Nick and said, "Jessie just had her first workout with me."

"Oh, nice to meet you." Nick held his hand out and Jessie took it, but Mackenzie thought she caught a glimpse of annoyance before she did.

"I'm going to get that shower. If you change your mind about dinner..." She smiled again, leaving Mackenzie with no doubt she was indeed coming on to her.

Jessie walked away, leaving Mackenzie and Nick to stare after her. Nick found his voice first. "What the hell was that?"

"I was just about to ask you the same thing," Mackenzie said, still looking toward the shower.

"That was about as blatant a come-on as I've ever seen. And right in front of me too." Nick frowned. "You haven't told anyone besides your mother, have you?"

"Only Palmer, and she's so happy I'm finally divorcing you she wouldn't do anything to put that in jeopardy. By the way, you are more than a little late. You were supposed to be here two hours ago."

"Sorry." Nick bent down and kissed her cheek. "But if you ask me, it looked like I got here too early. So you gonna hit it?"

Mackenzie put some weight behind the punch she landed on Nick's shoulder. "You're on your own. I have some paperwork to do. Rack your weights when you're done and don't blast the music."

Mackenzie was halfway to her office when Nick called out to her. "Don't forget about tomorrow. I made reservations for seven thirty at that French place my mother likes."

She gave him a "how could I forget" look and continued toward her office.

"Hey? Are you sure you want to do this, Mackenzie? I mean, you know I'm fine with the way things are." Nick had his workout towel twisted between his hands. Mackenzie recognized the anxiety on his face. She had known Nick for a long time. He was one of her best friends. He'd been there when her mother couldn't be, and he had given her a gift worth the peace of mind she had afforded him the last few years. But she needed her own life. She could tell by the look on his face that he understood that.

"I wish I could be, Nick, but I just can't live like that anymore. You know I'll always—"

Nick's sudden grin shut off her next words. "I know. I just thought I would check."

Mackenzie smiled back, though a little less exuberantly, and continued to her office. They both knew this was the right thing to do. Living a lie was never a good idea, but this was going to be painful. Despite Nick's best efforts, she was sure Barb and Arnult Copeland would make sure of that.

❖

Her paperwork sat untouched as Mackenzie's thoughts vacillated between her dreaded dinner with her in-laws and, of course, Colby.

She was pulled from her thoughts by the feeling of being watched. She looked up expecting to see Nick in the doorway.

Her new client, Jessie, was standing in the doorway dressed in a short white shirt and skirt that showed off her long legs.

Mackenzie had to tear her eyes away from the woman's bare midriff. "Jessie, hi. Did you have a question?" Weights clanked over the sound of Nick's bass-laden workout music.

"Yeah, I thought I would check in to make sure you hadn't worked up an appetite while I was in the shower."

Mackenzie put her pen down and studied Jessie. She was certainly attractive enough, and Mackenzie should have felt flattered, but there was something off about this woman. She was trying way too hard. It was as if she wouldn't take no for an answer. Although she hadn't been in the market for a girlfriend for several years, Mackenzie had not been able to pick up a woman outside of an openly gay setting since she had left the military. Things like that didn't happen to her, but then neither did things like making love to your high school crush in a gym locker room. *Yeah, and look how well that turned out.*

"If you change your mind, you have my number on the paperwork." Jessie's smile as she turned to go said she fully expected Mackenzie to change her mind, and that annoyed Mackenzie enough to push her into action.

"Um, Jessie?"

"Yeah?" Jessie turned around with a smile wide with confidence, and it was starting to get on Mackenzie's nerves. "I'm married, and even if I wasn't, I don't date clients."

The smile faded, and Jessie nodded her head in a touché motion. Mackenzie picked up her pen and would have gone back to her paperwork had she not suddenly focused on the pen in her hand. She dropped the pen on her desk and opened her hands palm side up. She had the sudden vision of herself between Colby's legs, holding her thighs apart as she tried to drown out the memories of how much of an idiot she had been to her when they were in school. Mackenzie heard Nick call out a cheery good-bye. If Jessie responded, she didn't hear it. She hadn't been tempted by that woman.

So why had she thrown caution to the wind with Colby? She had risked so much for one damn night. Mackenzie rubbed her forehead. She hadn't been thinking it was one night. She had been hoping for more and taking what she could get while she could. It was one of the things she had hoped she'd fixed about herself, and yet one look, one glimpse of the past and she was that scared little girl lashing out at the first thing that wouldn't hurt her back.

Damn it, Mackenzie, you were supposed to be past this. Mackenzie felt sorrow creep up on her, and she yearned for a hug from her favorite person in the world. *If you can't handle a one-night stand, how are you going to stand up to Nick's parents when they find out about the divorce?* The thought was enough to make her want to cry. She needed to get home. She needed to be reminded why, no matter what, it was all worth it.

Mackenzie was sitting slumped forward with her forehead cradled in her hands when the phone on her desk rang. Mackenzie scowled at the LED. She didn't recognize the number, and it was well after eight o'clock. She was justified in letting voicemail pick up. Her mother was notorious for leaving her cell phone on the counter at home. What if she was using a friend's phone? If something was wrong and Mackenzie was sitting there and didn't pick up, she would never be able to forgive herself.

"Fit Life, this is Mackenzie."

"Hey."

Mackenzie recognized Colby's voice but didn't answer right away. All the anxiety and turmoil she was feeling lifted. "Hey, you," she said softly.

"I'm surprised you're still at work on a Friday night."

"I had some paperwork to get done. Long hours are the one drawback to owning your own business." Colby's chuckle made Mackenzie smile.

"I know exactly what you mean. I'm also a business owner."

"How did you get my number?"

Colby hesitated. "Lara told me about your gym at the reunion."

"Oh." Mackenzie started to say something, changed her mind, but at the last minute decided to push forward. "I'm surprised to hear from you."

"Really? Why?"

Mackenzie paused, unsure of how much she was exposing herself by telling Colby she knew how long it had been since she had heard from her. "It's been almost a week."

"I know. I'm sorry. I've been working crazy hours."

"Are you working now?"

"I wouldn't call talking to you working. But yeah, I'm supposed to be."

"Good to know I'm not the only one working late on a Friday night."

"Nope, I guess not. I'd much rather be in your gym than where I am now, though."

"You don't look like you lack time for the gym."

Mackenzie heard the smile in Colby's voice. "Thank you for saying so. I started in college. I love it. It helps a lot with the job stress."

"What exactly do you do?" Colby didn't speak for a long moment, and Mackenzie rushed to apologize. "I'm sorry. I didn't mean to pry. You just mentioned how stressful it was."

"No, that's okay. I have a security firm. Ninety percent of my company's business is dealing with corporate issues. Security breaches in software, employee embezzlement, things of that nature."

"I should have known you would end up doing something with computers. You were so into them in high school." Mackenzie almost kicked herself for bringing up high school.

"I didn't think you knew anything about me." Colby's voice had gone soft with surprise. Mackenzie pictured her sitting behind a desk much neater than her own.

"I knew some things. Colby, I'm so sorry. I didn't know how to communicate with people back then."

"Please don't keep apologizing. It really wasn't a big deal."

Mackenzie clamped her jaw shut. It was a big deal to her. She had done damage. Colby had always been someone she wanted to get to know, and she had probably ruined any chance of that now. Another one of her many bad decisions.

"What are you doing right now?" Although she didn't seem in any hurry to get off the phone, Mackenzie thought Colby sounded a little tired.

"I'm just sitting in my office working on some paperwork. What about you?"

"I'm working too. Looking through a window, wishing I were somewhere else."

"Anyplace special?"

Colby chuckled. "Maybe."

Mackenzie smiled in response to the flirtation in Colby's tone.

"So what does one wear when one is a gym owner?"

Mackenzie looked down at her mismatched top and shorts. "I can't speak for other gym owners, but I wear color coordinated booty shorts with matching tank tops."

"Oh really?" Colby really did laugh now. "Your shoes match too?"

Mackenzie stuck out her dirty New Balance and nodded. "Oh yeah, they definitely match. So does the little emblem on my ankle socks. The whole ensemble is striking. Too bad you can't see me."

Colby's laughter was doing wonderful things to Mackenzie's insides. Finally Colby calmed down and sighed. "I bet you look fantastic."

Mackenzie didn't know what to say to that statement.

"What about your hair? Do you have it down or pulled back?"

"Um, down," Mackenzie said as she snatched the bandana off her head and tossed it on the floor so that her hair cascaded around her shoulders.

Colby uttered a breathless "Lovely" that made Mackenzie shiver.

"How about you? What are you wearing?"

"Business suit."

"Pants or skirt?"

"Skirt. Um, a very short skirt."

Something about the way she answered made Mackenzie think Colby was stretching the truth too. "Very short, huh?"

"Mmm-hmm, and heels."

Mackenzie smiled imagining Colby's calves in those heels and then she remembered what it had felt like to have those calves clamped down on her shoulder blades, and her face heated.

"What are you thinking right now?"

Colby sounded so clear it was easy for Mackenzie to imagine she was standing right next to her. "I was thinking about how it felt to have your legs on my shoulders."

The long silence made Mackenzie put her hand to her forehead and mouth "damn it." But Colby said softly, "I haven't been able to get that off my mind."

Mackenzie felt her heart leap with hope. "So is there anything we can do about it?"

"About what?"

"This thing between us. I thought maybe we could find out where it might lead."

Colby went quiet again, and when she spoke, she sounded as if she were standing in front of a pane of glass. Mackenzie imagined her looking out into the city lights with the phone pressed to her ear. The thought alone sent a flush of arousal throughout her body.

"I don't know if seeing you is a good idea, Mackenzie."

"Why not?"

"Because I'm still thinking about what we did the last time."

"Is that bad?"

"It is when I wake up sweating or when I'm meeting with clients and all I can think about is how you felt on my fingertips."

Mackenzie inhaled, closed her eyes, and reveled in that memory too.

"Your eyes are closed, aren't they?"

"How did you know?"

"Don't open them. Keep them closed. Imagine I'm there with you."

"Okay." Mackenzie obediently closed her eyes.

"Can you, would you open your legs for me?"

"Yes."

Colby's breath quickened. "Do you touch yourself when you think of me?"

Mackenzie swallowed, licked her lips. "I have."

"How many times?"

"Four, I think. I...I was having a hard time getting to sleep."

"And touching yourself helped?" Colby asked.

"Yes."

"Would you do me a favor?"

"Anything," Mackenzie said without hesitation.

"Would you touch yourself now? Would you imagine it's me there with you?"

Mackenzie opened her eyes and stared into the darkness outside her window. "Colby, I—"

"I'm sorry. I don't know what I was thinking."

"Don't apologize. Can you give me a second?" Mackenzie set the phone on the desk and walked to her door, closed it, and turned the lock. She would have gone straight back to her desk, to Colby waiting on the phone, but a flicker of light at the window reminded her she should probably close her blinds. She used the wand to slant them down and picked up the phone.

"Colby?"

"Mackenzie?"

"What do you want me to do?"

Colby made no effort to hide her inhale, and Mackenzie imagined Colby's lips on her neck and shoulder.

"Are you sitting at your desk?" Colby's question was an intimate hum in her ear.

"Yes," Mackenzie said.

"Turn away from it."

"But there's a window."

"It's closed, isn't it? No one can see you, can they?"

Mackenzie did as she was told and spun the chair away from her desk and the pile of paperwork on it. "Okay."

"Promise you'll keep your eyes closed too?"

"I promise."

"If I were there, I'd want to touch your breasts. I'd want to cup them in my hands. Can you do it for me? Tell me what they feel like?"

Mackenzie trapped the phone between her ear and shoulder, leaving her hands free to cover her breasts. Her nipples hardened at the thought of Colby touching her this way.

"Are they hard?"

"From the moment I realized it was you on the other end of the line."

"Are you rubbing them?"

"Yes."

"If I were there, I'd kiss you right now. I know your lips are parted. I can tell by the way you're breathing. I'd stand right between your legs and I'd kiss you until you begged me to stop."

Mackenzie opened her legs, imagining Colby standing there.

"Mackenzie?" Colby's voice hitched. "Would you take your sports bra off for me?"

Mackenzie hooked a thumb in the space between her breasts and would have ripped the sports bra over her head, but something told her to slow down, to draw the moment out. She slowly removed one arm and then the other before easing the bra up and over her breasts. "Okay, it's off," she said shyly. She dropped it on the floor and leaned back against the cool leather of her chair.

Mackenzie cupped her breasts, feeling the hard nipples in her palms, and imagined it was Colby's hands holding her. "I wish I had kissed your breasts." Colby gasped, and Mackenzie imagined her standing behind her, kissing and cupping her breasts. "They're perfect."

Mackenzie smiled. "How do you know how perfect they are?"

Colby was silent. "I can tell just by looking at you. I wanted to touch them the minute I saw you. I wanted to kiss your navel, run my tongue all over your body until you begged me to stop."

Colby was igniting a fire in her body so deep Mackenzie had to close her legs to keep it contained. "Open your legs, Mackenzie."

Mackenzie instantly opened her legs and squeezed her eyes tight despite them already being closed. "Colby, we're going to have to slow down. I'm already—"

"It's okay. Pull your shorts down." Colby's voice sounded muffled, soft, aroused, heated, excited, all of the things Mackenzie herself felt. "Imagine I'm there with you, touching you." Mackenzie understood Colby was giving her an order, so she complied. "I wouldn't use too much pressure, I'd be very gentle with you. Can you open wider for me, Mackenzie?"

Mackenzie nodded, remembered Colby wasn't there, and then let out a breathless, "Yes." Her chair groaned as she opened her legs as wide as she could. Air teased her dampness, and she imagined Colby looking at her center.

"You have no idea how much I want to touch you. If I were there, I'd kiss those beautiful thighs of yours until neither of us could stand it. Then I'd kiss you on your lips and I'd use my tongue."

Mackenzie used the very tip of her fingers to do as Colby described. "If you have arms on that chair, can you put your legs up on them?" Mackenzie did as she was told but had temporarily lost her ability to speak. Colby must have assumed she would obey because soon after Mackenzie complied Colby breathed, "My God, you look so good. Would you like me to kiss you?"

"Yes, please."

"I would kiss you down there. I'd run my tongue along the shaft of your clit." Mackenzie whimpered as she lost herself in the sound of Colby's voice. "I'd capture your clit between my lips and I'd lavish your clit with my tongue." Mackenzie moved her mouth away from the phone. She was almost gasping now. She pictured the aroused look on Colby's face when she had brought her to orgasm at the reunion.

"I bet you are so wet right now, Mackenzie. I bet if I wanted to slip one finger inside you I could easily do that, couldn't I?"

"Yes."

"I'd really like to do that. Would it be all right with you?"

"Oh God, yes," Mackenzie said, and she thought she heard Colby turn away from the phone and groan.

"Tell me what I'm missing," Colby said and Mackenzie slipped one finger into heat caused by the woman she had secretly wanted for years.

"I'm wet and I...I'm already close. It feels like if I'm not careful—"

Colby interrupted her. "I don't want you to come. Not yet."

"Okay," Mackenzie said and bit her bottom lip.

"Take your finger out."

Mackenzie protested.

"Please, Mackenzie."

"Okay." Mackenzie slowly eased out of herself and felt moisture trickle from her and between her ass cheeks. "Put them into your mouth. Tell me what you taste like."

Mackenzie ran her tongue over her bottom lip and then put

her wet fingers in her mouth and almost groaned. Her body jerked as her mind flashed back to the memory of Colby's face and body as she contorted in pleasure. Mackenzie had gloried in the taste and the feel of her in her mouth.

"Tell me," Colby ordered.

"I taste like you. Like you did. Both sweet and salty and…"

"And what?"

"And sex. I taste like want and need and…"

"Put them back."

Mackenzie did so, quickly separating the lips of her vagina so her engorged clitoris was exposed to the cooling air and standing proud. She ran her finger up one side and down the other and then flattened it before moving it swiftly up and down.

"Two fingers inside. Now."

Mackenzie obeyed, gasped, jerked, and almost came, but she closed her legs around her own hand in an effort to keep the flood at bay.

"Don't close your legs, Mackenzie. Let me in." Colby sounded as if she were choking.

Mackenzie placed her legs over the arms of the chair and threw her head back with the phone still tucked between her ear and shoulder. She imagined Colby thrusting into her, toes curled, and she fought off the impending orgasm. A soft gasp was the only sound she heard for several minutes as she thrust, pulling back slowly and then reentering herself repeatedly until her legs felt as if they were not part of her body and her hips were lifting off the chair.

Mackenzie murmured Colby's name, and her lower body jerked. "Colby," she said again, and then she was done. Her body locked down hard on her fingers. She thought she heard Colby tell her it was okay, but she fought just like she always had when given an easy out. She tried to hold off, tried to force the end away but couldn't. She arched into the fingers and then felt the orgasm slam into her so hard she didn't have the energy to keep the phone tucked in its place. She heard it drop to the floor as her body rocked back one last time and she sank down over her fingers lost in the orgasm and an image of Colby's face as she had brought her to hers.

❖

"Are you still there?"

"Of course I am," Colby said through lips sore from biting. Her breath created a ghostly plume on the outside of Mackenzie's window that disappeared slowly. She should have been ashamed, but she wasn't. She was far too aroused to allow guilt to intrude. Maybe if Mackenzie had taken Jessie up on her offer, it would have been easier to turn away. She could have gone back to the Copelands and told them what they wanted to hear. Jessie had come highly recommended by a private investigator who specialized in infidelity cases. Colby could tell from the miffed expression on the woman's face when she'd left the gym that she wasn't used to being turned down.

Colby would have to figure out a way to let Mackenzie know how little privacy window blinds offered. Anyone with an inclination could walk up outside her window and do as she had—peer through the tiny little oblong holes in the slats. The moment insecurity began to steal over Mackenzie, Colby knew it.

"I'm sorry if you feel we went too far," Colby said. Her hand went to the window to touch it, but she jerked it back down to her side.

"Don't say sorry. It's not you. It's just been an odd day."

"You mean you don't have phone sex with a near stranger every day?" *Damn it all, why do I feel so guilty?* Even if what the Copelands said wasn't true, Mackenzie could have put a stop to this at any time. None of this was her fault. *That's right. You were just the one standing out here with your forehead pressed up against the window like a Peeping Tom.*

"Unfortunately, no. I don't often get the opportunity to have phone sex with a gorgeous woman."

Mackenzie was smiling now, and Colby could have looked at her forever. But Mackenzie turned around and faced her desk so all Colby saw was the top of her head and one slender hand plucking nervously at the upholstery of the chair.

"I would think women would come on to you all the time." It was a stupid statement. But it was one that would allow Mackenzie to admit that she was married, admit something, but of course she didn't. Colby's emotions slid from disappointment with Mackenzie for not being honest to anger at herself for wishing she could trust her. What difference did it make if Mackenzie told the truth? The woman *was* married. That's all there was to it.

"No, I...well, it's funny, but I had a new client today and she kind of made it obvious she was interested."

Colby bit her bottom lip. Jessie *had* made it obvious. She had done everything but tackle Mackenzie to the ground and sit on her face. That was what Colby had hired her to do. Nobody was more surprised than Colby was when Jessie had come out of the building frustrated and sure that Mackenzie was not gay. Colby flashed back to the reunion and Mackenzie's talented tongue but didn't answer. She should have walked the block and a half to her car and driven away. She should have called the Copelands and told them...what? That their daughter-in-law wasn't gay? That would be a lie. She was definitely gay.

"So she wasn't your type? That's assuming you didn't take her up on her offer."

"You assume correctly. I wouldn't say she wasn't my type."

"I heard a 'but' in there." Colby stared at the back of Mackenzie's head but got no clue to what was going on in her mind until she spoke.

"I don't sleep around, Colby. I know this is probably hard for you to believe after what we did at the reunion and just now, but I haven't been with anyone in a long time."

"Just stop, okay?" Colby didn't know where the burst of

anger came from, but for some reason she couldn't bear the thought of Mackenzie lying to her.

"What did I say?"

"Nothing. I just want to see you." *Damn it all to hell.* She needed to get this woman out of her head so she could move on with her life. Screw the Copelands and their money. This was beyond that. She had messed up badly by getting involved with Mackenzie, and the only way she knew to make it better was to tell Mackenzie the truth. "I *need to* see you, Mackenzie. Do you want to see me?" she asked, but her thoughts were racing in a different direction. *Tell me no, Mackenzie. Tell me you're married and you made a mistake. Tell me you don't want me the way that I want you, that it's all a game.*

"When?" With one word, Mackenzie managed to both break Colby's heart and fill it with hope.

"Tomorrow. I can be there around eight o'clock. Same hotel I was at during the reunion." Seeing Mackenzie again was a mistake, Colby knew that, but she needed to figure this thing out. She needed to figure out what her tie to this woman was. Otherwise, she wouldn't be able to get her off her mind. Maybe it was just the sex. It had to be just the sex. But she had never been one to get involved with straight women, especially married women with in-laws like the Copelands. That was just asking for trouble. Wasn't it?

"I can't," Mackenzie said.

Colby swallowed. "You can't or don't want to?"

"I'm sorry. I have an appointment tomorrow night and it's not something I can get out of."

Colby swallowed. "Okay, what about after your appointment?"

Mackenzie sounded doubtful. "I don't know how long it'll take."

Maybe she really doesn't want to see me. Colby was so disappointed by that possibility that it soured her. *This is not good.* "Look, never mind."

"Don't say that. I'm not trying to brush you off. I've been

thinking about you all week," Mackenzie said. "If I could get out of this appointment, believe me, I would."

"I believe you," Colby said and felt her mouth stretch into a goofy smile. She felt like she was a teenager with her first crush.

"Good. You're smiling, aren't you?" Mackenzie asked.

"Yes. You?"

"Maybe."

"Why maybe?"

"It depends on your answer to my next question."

"Okay, ask."

"Did your client turn you on? The one who came on to you? Is that why you…?"

"No. Not at all. I was only thinking about you."

Colby sighed. She might have said something silly like "good," but a door opened and shocked her back to reality. "I'll call you tomorrow from the hotel," she said and hung up.

Colby tried to lean back into the shadows, but she could tell by the way Nick Copeland hesitated and walked toward her that he had already seen her. "Damn, damn, damn," Colby whispered and then squatted down and acted like she was retching.

"Hey, you all right?" Nick sounded so concerned that Colby was surprised. She doubted either of his parents would have bothered to check on the welfare of a stranger.

"Yeah, I'm fine. Just a little stomach thing."

"Okay, well, you're not driving, are you?" Nick asked suspiciously. Colby would rather he think she was wasted than doing what she had been doing—peeping at his wife while she had phone sex with her. *Damn it all.*

"No, I'm okay." Colby stood, careful to keep her face tilted down.

Colby glanced up and caught a glimpse of Nick's dimpled chin and thick, wavy hair. Nick Copeland seemed a little too carefree for someone like Mackenzie. She had changed a lot in ten years, but there was still an element of intensity about her.

"Look, can I call someone for you? Maybe take you somewhere?"

"I'm fine. Just something I ate."

Nick was still frowning when Colby started to back away from him.

"Are you from around here?" he asked, stopping her retreat and her heart cold.

Colby recovered quickly. "Just here on business. Thanks for your concern, but I'll be fine." Colby turned and started walking away. She would have to double back to her car. She turned the corner and risked a glimpse back just in time to see Nick look at the window of Mackenzie's office and then in her direction. Damn it, what was it about this woman that made her lose her mind? She had almost been caught peeping, and for what? Colby blinked, too afraid to answer her own question. This was getting ridiculous. She needed to end this thing. She needed to give the Copelands their information or tell them to go to hell. She needed to get away from Mackenzie Brandt before she forgot why she'd ever hated her in the first place.

❖

Mackenzie and Nick walked into the restaurant side by side. Two warriors joined together in combat. As expected, Nick's parents had already been seated, and from the slack-jawed look in Barb's face, she had already had several of her drink of choice—martinis so dry the fumes alone made Mackenzie cough.

"Oh, excellent, my mother looks like she's already three sheets to the wind." Nick had perfected the art of speaking without moving his lips.

Mackenzie nodded. "Looks that way, but don't get cocky yet."

Nick might have known his parents longer, but between the two of them, he was always more optimistic. He had insisted his parents would be happy when they told them four years ago that they were getting married. He had been wrong about that. Mackenzie followed Nick to the table feeling unusually weary and willing to allow Nick to jump into the lion's den first.

"Good evening, Mother, Father." Nick kissed his mother's cheek and shook his father's hand.

Mackenzie kissed Barb's dust-dry cheek and tried not to cough as the fumes from Barb's tumbler burned the inside of her nostrils. Mackenzie bussed her father-in-law's cheek and asked him about his golf game. As expected, the golf question broke the ice and Arnult launched into an amusing story. Mackenzie knew it was supposed to be amusing because Arnult laughed through most of it. She tried to chuckle, but she failed. Barb glanced at her over the rim of her tumbler. Barb was the real viper of this pair. Quiet, unpredictable, and deadly. Luckily, her only weakness was readily available. Mackenzie caught the waiter as he walked by.

"Would you please bring me a tall water with a lime and another drink for my mother-in-law?" Mackenzie looked at Barb as if to ask permission, and as expected, Barb nodded her approval. She thanked the waiter and turned to smile at Barb. Her smile was not returned.

"Your shoulders are getting too large to wear a sleeveless dress, dear."

Mackenzie looked down at her dress, purchased specifically for this occasion because Nick had said pants might antagonize his mother unnecessarily.

"Well, muscles kind of come with my profession."

"I think Mackenzie looks fantastic, Mother."

Mackenzie looked at Nick, surprised he would take up for her on such a mundane point when he had left her to fend for herself on more important points in the past.

"Well, in my day women were content to look like women." This was said with a haughtiness that would have rankled if Mackenzie didn't know it was about to get much, much worse.

"Things have changed since our day, Barb. Let Mackenzie

be." Now it was Arnult's turn to surprise her. The waiter returned with their drinks and asked if they were ready to order. Barb informed him that they were, seemingly unconcerned that neither Mackenzie nor Nick had looked at their menus.

Mackenzie listened as Barb and Arnult ordered, and she quickly scanned the menu. Nick would order his usual. A pasta dish of some sort, drowning in cream or cheese.

"Nick, darling, you on the other hand, look as if you are putting on a bit of fat." The table went quiet. "Why don't you try the Nicoise salad? It's wonderful and they don't put many potatoes in it."

The waiter stood at Barb's side, pen poised. A gambit of emotions played across Nick's handsome face. Like always, she was rooting for him, wanting him to stand up to his parents, even for something as unimportant as what he ate for dinner.

"You're right, Mother. A Nicoise salad sounds good."

Mackenzie lost her appetite and ordered a cup of onion soup and a side salad.

The waiter scurried away with their order, and Mackenzie sipped at her water. Now was a good time to launch into the unpleasant discussion. As much as Barb felt it was perfectly okay to embarrass her son in front of others, she would never embarrass herself, which was why Mackenzie and Nick had asked his parents to meet them here. The restaurant was known for speedy service, so if they timed it correctly they could be in and out in an hour. Mackenzie's thoughts flashed on Colby waiting for her in the hotel, but she quickly yanked herself back to the unpleasant task at hand.

"Barb, Arnult, we asked you here because we need to tell you something."

Barb turned drab blue eyes on Mackenzie but said nothing.

Mackenzie swallowed, and to her surprise Nick took her hand on the table as a show of solidarity. Or was he just bracing himself?

"There's no easy way to say this," Mackenzie said. "So I'm

just going to say it and hope you give me—us—the chance to explain."

"We're getting a divorce," Nick blurted, and Mackenzie stiffened and looked from Arnult to Barb.

Instead of appearing shocked, Nick's parents showed very little emotion. "Have you thought about your career?" Arnult asked.

"Accountants get divorced all the time," Nick said.

"He means your political aspirations," Barb said, and her tone made Mackenzie want to yell, "April fools," and run out of the restaurant.

"Mother, I'm not even sure I want to go into politics."

"Your grandfather used to say the same thing. It has a way of calling to the men in our family." Mackenzie waited for Barb to finish her third drink before she spoke.

"It's not just up to Nick, Barb. We decided together the marriage wasn't working."

"What about Olivia?" Barb asked.

Mackenzie had expected this question before the question about Nick's career. The fact that their granddaughter was almost an afterthought did nothing to endear these people to her. *You should have thought about that before you married into the family.*

"Olivia is too young to understand, Barb. But when she's old enough we'll tell her the truth. That we love each other, but we made a wonderful mistake getting married. Wonderful because we had her, but a mistake because as much as we love each other, we aren't in love with each other." Mackenzie looked at Nick and returned his smile.

"That's the gist of it," he said as the waiter appeared with their salads, forestalling any comebacks Barb had planned.

The waiter walked away and Barb said, "All of you young women are so hot to become single parents. Parenting is a great responsibility."

Mackenzie bit the inside of her cheek to keep from saying,

Unless you can afford a full-time live-in nanny until they are old enough to ship off to boarding school.

Barb was still speaking. "You can't just go out and see who you want to see and do what you want to do. You just remember that while you're talking about a divorce. Children are impressionable." Barb's gaze never wavered, and Mackenzie had the uncomfortable idea that Barb had somehow found out about the reunion, or the cab, or Lord help her—the phone sex.

"I'm not going anywhere, Mother. I'm still Olivia's father. And you two are still her grandparents. She'll still have the same parents. We just won't be living under the same roof."

The other restaurant customers laughed and had conversations over their meals while Mackenzie's table ate in almost silence. This might possibly be the last time she had to deal with the uncomfortable presences of the Copelands in her life. The thought brought a surge of joy that weakened only when she glanced at Nick. He would never have the relief she had. Not until he came completely clean to them. As much as she loved Nick, she knew he would never willingly do that. Nick was weak where his parents were concerned. Mackenzie hoped her daughter never felt the need to lie about who she was in order to please *her*. Mackenzie looked up at the clock. It was already just past eight. She had told Colby she would be late, but how late was too late? She would try, no matter what. She needed to stave off the chill caused by Barb Copeland's glare.

CHAPTER SIX

Roheibeth Hotel

The tingle that began when the phone rang faded when Colby detected weariness in Mackenzie's hello. She wondered for the umptcenth time why she had allowed herself to get involved with this case. "Hi, where are you?"

"Downstairs in the parking lot."

"I understand if you're too tired to come up."

Truthfully, Colby wouldn't understand. During the drive to Roheibeth she had convinced herself she would see Mackenzie this one last time to get her out of her system. She couldn't lie to herself about this being like any other job anymore. Even the residual anger left over from high school had faded into something a lot more convoluted.

"I am a little tired."

It took Colby a moment to realize that her feelings were hurt because Mackenzie was too tired to see her when she was just downstairs and another moment to decide that if she were smart, she would come up with a reason to get off the phone and head back to Portland with her tail tucked, but still intact.

"I know it's late, but I hoped you'd still like me to come up. I've been looking forward to seeing you all day."

"It's not too late." Colby flushed with anger caused by

embarrassment at how eager she sounded. Anger didn't stop her from giving Mackenzie her room number, though. Colby hung up the phone and turned around to appraise her room. The bedclothes were turned back, a bottle of champagne slumped in a bucket of melting ice, and a plate of fruit sat untouched on a cart left by room service over an hour ago. Colby's hand went to her chest and then to her stomach when her fingertips touched bare skin. She looked down at the thick white bathrobe she was wearing and winced. Her intention had been to have something brought up in case Mackenzie hadn't eaten. When she hadn't heard anything by ten, she'd decided to soak her sore ego and rioting body in a hot bath and go to bed. Now it looked like she had planned what she really did hope would happen—an evening of sex sustained with food and more sex. But it was one thing to believe you were going to get some and another entirely to open the door in a robe, have a banquet set out and the damn bedclothes turned back. The only faux pas she hadn't made was popping some "let's fuck" music in the hotel's combo CD player/alarm clock.

The tentative knock on the door startled Colby. She looked toward the closet where she had stuck her suitcase. She would have to make Mackenzie stay outside while she found something in her luggage or put on the dirty clothes she had worn all day. Neither option felt like a good one, so Colby took a deep breath, opened the door, and almost keeled over. Mackenzie was wearing a dress. Colby had been wrong about how she would look in one. The black fabric fit Mackenzie's body, covering her hips and flat stomach like a glove, then dropping gracefully to an almost demure place at her calf.

Colby lingered on Mackenzie's legs, remembering how they had looked through the window. She wondered what they would feel like wrapped around her waist or over her shoulders. Colby realized she had been staring at Mackenzie far longer than was polite and forced a smile as she raised her gaze to Mackenzie's face. She only got so far as Mackenzie's neck and the soft tendrils of hair that brushed her shoulders. Colby parted her lips to say hello, but nothing came out. She wanted to run her lips along those wonderfully strong shoulders. In their first encounter, she hadn't had the opportunity to explore Mackenzie's body, and now...

"It's too much, isn't it?"

Colby looked up, startled. She had been standing in the door ogling Mackenzie like a virgin getting ready for first rights. From the look on Mackenzie's face, not only had she noticed, she was embarrassed. *Good job, idiot. So much for the sure thing.*

"Is what too much?" Colby asked as she tried to clear the pleasant fog from her brain.

"The dress. I was told that I was too muscular to go sleeveless."

"Oh good Lord! You aren't too muscular. That dress is fantastic. You look fantastic. You know some dumbasses, don't you?" Colby sputtered to a stop. Mackenzie's smile was almost worth feeling she had gone overboard.

"I'm glad you disagree. May I come in? It's drafty out here." Colby moved quickly out of the entryway to allow Mackenzie to pass. The dress from the back was almost as lovely as the front. Low cut, revealing the feminine ripple of Mackenzie's muscled back and ending at the swell of her backside. Colby remembered she was holding the door open and quickly shut it, blinking rapidly. Between this dress and the memory of Mackenzie pleasuring herself in her office, Colby would be lucky if she didn't end up with a sleep disorder. Of course if she was going to lay awake at night, she could think of a lot worse memories to be tormented by. What the hell happened to the tomboy she remembered from high school? The sweatshirts and baggy jeans were a lot easier to deal with. *You better be happy she didn't walk in here wearing her workout clothes. Matching or not, you'd be on the floor with your ass in the air.*

"I'm serious, by the way. You look gorgeous."

Mackenzie's smile warmed and soothed the nervous place in Colby's stomach.

"Thank you. You look lovely in that robe."

Embarrassment made Colby's armpits prickle. The robe was the usual thick terrycloth variety that hotels left for their guests' comfort in the hopes that they would then overindulge in the honor bar, throw caution to the wind, and pay three hundred bucks for the permanent use of the robe.

"I look like a marshmallow. I was just about to run a bath before you called."

"Really?" Mackenzie tilted her head to the side. "Care for some company?"

Colby's pulse sped up at the quiet way the question was asked. "I'd like that very much. Are you sure you're up to it? You said you were tired. Your prior engagement must have taken a lot out of you. I hope it was worth it."

Mackenzie looked surprised and then to Colby's surprise, she looked angry. "What difference does it make if I'm tired or not?"

"What? I just meant…"

"I know what you meant. I'm sorry for jumping down your throat. Yes, I'm tired, but I came here tonight to forget the mess I've made of my life. I don't want to be told that I look tired or that I work too much or…I came here to be…"

Colby clenched her jaw, and Mackenzie folded her arms in front of her chest. "You came here to be what?" Colby's anger flared, and this time there was no embarrassment to temper it. Mackenzie had no right to take her problems out on her. She was the one who should be angry. After all, she was the one who… "You came here to be what, Mackenzie?"

"I came here to be fucked, all right? I don't want to pretend like we…"

"Say it," Colby whispered.

"Like we aren't just using each other." Mackenzie's words fell between them like a stone in a still pond.

Colby swallowed. She felt as if she had just been pushed aside in a crowded hallway, and damn it all if it didn't hurt. She reached out and Mackenzie fell into her arms. Their kiss was brutal. Colby welcomed the sting of their lips melding. Welcomed it the way one welcomes a bite to the fist in the hopes that it will distract from a real, deeper pain.

Mackenzie's fingers were working desperately at the terrycloth knot tied at Colby's waist. Colby felt the briefest moment of uncharacteristic modesty when the knot loosened and her robe fell open. Mackenzie's kiss gentled, and when their mouths separated Mackenzie pressed her forehead to Colby's. Mackenzie's eyes scorched her body, caressing her, loving her without touching her. Colby melted when she heard the soft intake of breath.

"Dear God. You are beautiful," Mackenzie said, and Colby felt whatever vestiges of ice that had solidified around her heart over the last ten years melt. She tried to hold on to it by remembering Nick Copeland's annoyingly engaging smile. She managed to focus for a second, but when Mackenzie's trembling lips smoothed over hers, Nick Copeland was the furthest thing from Colby's mind. She didn't resist when Mackenzie urged her backward toward the bed. Colby welcomed the weight of her when they fell as one onto the bed.

Colby swam in a sea of balmy arousal, drifting on the pleasure that Mackenzie was bringing, blissfully cognizant that she was lying naked beneath a woman who, despite their history, she really didn't know. Vaguely, she realized she should be worried that she could think of nowhere else she would rather be.

Colby reached up and undid the clips that held Mackenzie's hair back, letting it cascade down upon her. Mackenzie's hip forced her legs wanton-wide.

"I'm ready," Colby said weakly in warning. "Your dress…"

"Screw the dress," Mackenzie said as she pressed down with her hips. Colby gasped in pleasure and reached up to grasp Mackenzie's ass to hold her in place. She couldn't believe how close she was already.

Mackenzie stopped moving. Colby would have protested,

but the words caught in her throat, imprisoned by the combination of mischievousness and arousal evident on Mackenzie's face. She sat up, her knees straddling Colby's hips. Her smile had lost some of its playfulness and now held an intensity that brought back memories of being cornered in a shower stall. *Anticipation. Damn...I felt it then too, but I was too scared to recognize it for what it was.*

"Put your hands up," Mackenzie ordered, and after a moment's hesitation, Colby did what she was told. She noticed that Mackenzie was holding the belt of her robe in her hands. "I'm going to tie your hands. You don't get to touch me. Only I get to touch you. Understood?"

Colby frowned. She understood, but she didn't like it one bit.

"Colby, I...may I have you tonight? Please? I just want to be able to forget how crappy life can be. Just for a little while."

"Okay," Colby said.

Mackenzie looked stunned. Colby couldn't quite figure out why. It wasn't as if they had never been together, but she spoke anyway just so she could keep that look of wonder on Mackenzie's face. "Tonight I'm yours. You can do or say whatever you want. Just let yourself go." Colby put her hands above her head and crossed them at the wrist. Mackenzie tied them with ceremonial carefulness.

Colby followed Mackenzie with her eyes as she stood and unzipped the dress, slipping the straps over her shoulders and down her arms.

Colby remembered the same look of subdued passion on Mackenzie's face as she had peered at her through the window. Colby clenched her fingers tight and her breath came out in a sharp gasp. The belt was knotted loosely. She could easily slip her hands out if she wanted.

The dress fell to the ground, pooling in a puddle of black fabric at Mackenzie's bare feet.

"Where are your panties?" Colby whispered in awe.

"I left them in my glove box. I got excited on the drive over." If Mackenzie hadn't looked slightly embarrassed, Colby would have believed the comment had been made specifically to garner a reaction. A hot flush of heat spread from the soles of Colby's feet to the top of her head.

The bed dipped as Mackenzie sat down, her hands intertwined and pressed demurely between her knees. Colby liked that Mackenzie didn't seem to be in any hurry and tried to calm her own nerves. She could be patient too. It wasn't like they were on a timer or anything. Mackenzie stood and reached for the bottle of champagne, water sloshed over the rim of the bucket, but Colby couldn't look away from Mackenzie's perfect apple-bottomed ass. Hell, her whole body was perfect, even down to the small silvery stretch marks that glistened at her sides. Colby wondered what they would feel like beneath her tongue. Mackenzie looked around for a towel. She found the small one Colby had left sitting on the small table and used it to twist the cork off the champagne. She smiled and held it over a glass, one brow raised.

"We celebrating something?" Colby asked, suddenly aware of her own body. She had been nude with women before, but certainly not displayed the way she was now. Mackenzie didn't answer, her gaze fixed firmly on Colby's chest, and she seemed lost in her own thoughts. Colby should have been embarrassed but wasn't. She lifted her chest a little, liking the way her nipples stood up proud and aroused. She could tell by the way Mackenzie licked her lips that she liked it too.

"You're going to spill," Colby said with a smile. Mackenzie jumped and straightened her listing glass as she walked closer to the bed, bringing her pelvis in line with Colby's head. Colby stared greedily, inhaled the scent of some type of citrus, and licked her lips.

"You thirsty?" Mackenzie asked softly.

"Yes, but not for champagne."

Mackenzie set the champagne glass down on the end table and stood above her with a half-smile on her face. "I can't believe I'm just standing in front of you like this."

"I was just thinking the same thing. I don't feel even remotely shy."

"Not even remotely?"

"Well, maybe a little."

Mackenzie took a sip of her champagne, her eyes roving over Colby's body as she did it. Remembering how it had made her heart leap into her throat when she had secretly watched Mackenzie through the window, Colby slowly stretched out her legs and opened them wide, stopping Mackenzie cold as she reached for a strawberry.

"You did that on purpose," Mackenzie whispered.

"I don't know what you mean." Colby shifted her hips in a figure eight, managing to arch her back and lick her lips at the same time. The strawberry fell from Mackenzie's hand and into her champagne glass with a plop.

"Oh shit." Colby laughed as Mackenzie blinked at the floating piece of fruit and tried to fish it out.

"You think that's funny?" Mackenzie pulled the strawberry out and brushed it along Colby's lips.

"I do think it's funny." Colby licked the drops off. "I do think I let the champagne chill too long. Sorry. I thought you weren't coming."

"Hmm, it's fine, see?" Mackenzie held her glass out and Colby arched up to sip from it. A small trail spilled from the side of her mouth. She would have slipped her hand from her binds to catch it, but Mackenzie said, "Let me."

Her lips warmed Colby's cheek first and then her tongue followed the chill of the champagne to her neck. Colby had always been cursed with a sensitive neck, but Mackenzie's touch was firm enough not to tickle and gentle enough to cause her body to arch in real pleasure this time. The bed shifted, and before another thought could cross Colby's mind, Mackenzie lay on top of her. There was a long, slow moment where their bodies settled into each other nipple to nipple, hip to hip. The length of Mackenzie's hair spilled down on Colby's face, temporarily blinding her. When Mackenzie finally looked up, the shocked look on her face was enough to tell Colby that she felt it too. Dread threatened to overcome arousal, but Colby arched up and Mackenzie blinked, breaking the spell. Colby rotated her hips beneath Mackenzie, urging her to move with her, telling her that it was okay with her kiss. Mackenzie cupped the back of Colby's shoulder blades and inserted herself between Colby's legs.

"Wait, I'll go quickly," Colby said.

"It's okay. I want you to."

Colby would have protested if she weren't already lost. Mackenzie's hands were at her hips urging her forward. Colby tried to pull back to make the moment last longer.

"Oh no, you don't," Mackenzie said and then she was gone. Colby began to protest, but the words dried in her throat. Mackenzie was gazing with rapt fascination between her legs. Colby tried to bring her knees together, feeling utterly exposed. The motion broke whatever spell Mackenzie was under because she looked up and the awe on her face caused Colby to forget about her embarrassment and anything else that wasn't named Mackenzie Brant.

"Beautiful," Mackenzie said in a voice husky with passion.

The first kiss was enough to make Colby lose it if she hadn't bitten her bottom lip as a distraction. When Mackenzie opened her mouth and took her in, clitoris and all, there was a moment when Colby thought Mackenzie was going to devour her whole. She welcomed it, yearned for it, opened her mouth to beg for it, but all that came out were sobs of pleasure. Just when she thought there could be no more peaks, Mackenzie stroked the opening to her vagina, asking for and receiving entry. The pleasure was so intense that she was no longer rolling her hips. Mackenzie was doing all the work, lifting and moving her at just the right pace. Mackenzie's face was shrouded with pleasure, and the muscles of her biceps flexed as she lifted Colby's body to the perfect angle. Colby heard her own raspy breathing momentarily suspend as the orgasm curled her toes, and she arched her back to an almost painful angle.

When Colby returned to her senses, she realized that Mackenzie was lying with her head on her hip but was holding her hand. Colby stirred when Mackenzie didn't look up as she expected. When she finally did, Colby gasped at how wanton Mackenzie looked. Her eyes were droopy with passion and her lips were full. Her face was damp from either sweat or Colby's desire. "I could do that forever," she said, and Colby felt something tug at her heart.

"Come up here." Mackenzie seemed reluctant to move. When she eased up the bed, she was about to lie down next to Colby. "No, all the way up."

Mackenzie frowned in confusion.

"I want to taste you too."

Mackenzie straddled Colby's chest, looking at her questioningly. "Come up a little bit," Colby said, and Mackenzie complied, bracing herself by grasping the headboard. Colby liked the way Mackenzie's stomach flexed when she moved. She liked the way the scent of her own musk mingled with the scent of Mackenzie's shampoo made her feel intoxicated. "Stop right there." Mackenzie froze.

"Come down lower," Colby ordered, and Mackenzie did so until Colby felt the silken warmth of Mackenzie on her chest. She slipped her hands from the belt and then around Mackenzie's small waist. "You're beautiful too. I've always thought you were beautiful." Colby arched her back, held her breasts close to Mackenzie, and rubbed her hard nipples along the sides of Mackenzie's clitoris. They both moaned simultaneously and Colby closed her legs to stop the pulsing that had started there. Her breasts were glistening from the evidence of Mackenzie's arousal. The scent in the air was intoxicating. Mackenzie had acted as if she hadn't expected her to reciprocate. She had been wrong. There was nothing Colby wanted more.

Colby reached behind her, moved the pillows into place, and glanced briefly up at Mackenzie's face, now infused with pleasure. "Come here, Mackenzie."

The first touch of tongue on lips shocked them both, but Mackenzie recovered faster and her hips began the age-old rocking motion. Her breath came in short gasps that got louder when Colby parted her outer lips for the soft, delicate skin. At first, Colby was careful not to use her teeth, but she could tell Mackenzie liked it when she did. She massaged and cradled Mackenzie's ass, loving the way her butt cheeks flexed and strained beneath her hands. A fine sheen of sweat covered them both and the sounds of their damp bodies coming together mingled with Mackenzie's soft cries.

Colby lifted her head and drove her tongue ever deeper into Mackenzie as the tip of her finger sought another opening, one less eager to accept her. Mackenzie's body stiffened, but she didn't pull away. Colby waited patiently for several seconds, gently stroking, quietly waiting, and soon Mackenzie was arching and taking her in with a gusto that meant she was in the throes of an orgasm. Colby curled both finger and tongue. Mackenzie's cry hit the ceiling and bounced back onto them. The sight of Mackenzie mesmerized her, every muscle tensed, hair wild about her head and mouth open in ecstasy.

❖

Mackenzie lay behind Colby tracing a path down her jawline with the pad of her thumb while her other arm was imprisoned beneath Colby's head. Colby belonged tucked into the curve of her body. She couldn't help but think if she said anything it would break the spell and the real world would come in and tear them apart.

"What are you thinking?" Colby asked in a lazy whisper.

"I was thinking that if someone had told me in high school that we would end up like this, I wouldn't have believed them."

Colby laughed. "You would have punched their lights out."

Mackenzie smiled. "I doubt that. I might have threatened it."

"Huh, well, I don't doubt it."

"Colby, I know I gave you a hard time back then. It's no excuse, but I didn't know how to talk to people."

"You seemed to do just fine with everyone but me." Mackenzie sensed no accusation behind Colby's words. If anything, she sounded drowsy, at peace, satiated, which was exactly how Mackenzie felt. *Let it go. All you have to do is drift off, lose yourself in the scent, feel, and memory of being with Colby.* All of it would be over soon enough. Colby would leave tomorrow. If she bothered to keep in touch, it wouldn't last long, and eventually their relationship would dwindle to nothing. Relationship? It wasn't a relationship. It was just sex. Wasn't it?

"That's not true, Colby."

"What's not true?"

All she had to do was be quiet. Colby would be asleep soon. "I had a hard time talking to almost everyone, but most of all you."

Colby went quiet for so long that Mackenzie thought she had fallen asleep. She went on because she had to get it all out. She had to put the words out there or keep pretending. "I was too young to understand my feelings. I had a crush on you, Colby. I didn't want to be gay. My dad…my dad always said that gay people were sick. So I thought what I felt when I saw you was wrong. Colby?"

Mackenzie shifted and looked down at Colby. Her light lashes dusted her cheeks and her breathing had evened into the cadence of sleep. Mackenzie relaxed. Just as well. Colby probably couldn't care less about her messed-up childhood and even more messed-up adulthood. The one thing—the only thing—she had going for her was at home tucked away from it all. That was the one thing she was grateful for. She'd made many mistakes, but with luck, her child would never have to know about them.

❖

Colby awakened when she felt Mackenzie ease out of bed before sunup. She pretended to be in a deep sleep. She hadn't meant to fall asleep on Mackenzie, but if she were being honest, she wasn't looking forward to a deep conversation. If Mackenzie started to be honest she would feel obligated to be honest too, and she wasn't ready to say good-bye. Not yet.

Colby heard Mackenzie enter the bathroom, but she continued to lie completely still. She knew she was a fool for not getting up, for not apologizing, for falling asleep on Mackenzie, but something kept her pinned to the bed. No, not just something. The sight of Mackenzie had made her a little too happy. A little too willing to forget that she was the same person who had tormented her in high school. The same person who was willing to make love to her, despite being married to someone else. The shower shut off, and Colby's apprehension skyrocketed. No, not make love. What they had been doing wasn't making love. Was it? How the hell would she know?

But she's divorcing him.

Does that make it all right?

Since when did I become such a prude?

I wasn't the one that took a vow. Why should I care if Mackenzie is willing to cheat on her husband?

But I do care. And that's a problem.

Colby was grateful her hair was just long enough to hide her face. She heard Mackenzie sit down at the table and the sound of scratching as she wrote out a note. Colby was almost relieved that Mackenzie was leaving. She felt too confused and guilty to look at her right now. Colby felt, rather than heard, Mackenzie approach the bed and pictured her standing there in that wonderful black dress, shoes in hand, hair down, and…what expression on her face? Colby didn't move as Mackenzie's lips feathered across the corner of her mouth. Colby clenched her fists beneath the covers, refusing to react despite her brain screaming at her to stop being a coward and to ask Mackenzie why she was leaving so early. She lay completely still as Mackenzie's presence dissipated. The door opened and there was a long, silent pause. She imagined Mackenzie looking back at her before the door eased shut.

❖

Mackenzie walked into her home and didn't stop until she reached a small bedroom at the end of the hall. She stood in the doorway and looked at the small figure huddled beneath the covers. Mackenzie smiled for the first time since waking up intertwined with Colby. Olivia was afraid of the dark. She had somehow decided that keeping the covers over her head kept her safe from whatever monsters hid in the shadows. At first, Mackenzie feared she would suffocate, but her mother had assured her that Olivia would be fine. When Mackenzie made the decision to have a baby, her first thought was for the health of her child. For the first time in her life she started looking at her own health. If not for Olivia she might never have turned her love of fitness into her life's work. Mackenzie's smile faded. Olivia was proof that her father was wrong. She wasn't a complete fuckup, or a failure. A failure could never make someone so perfect.

Mackenzie's next stop was at her mother's room. The door had been left open for Olivia, though the child usually slept hard once she went down. Now that she was home, she reached in to pull the door shut. "I'm awake," her mother said though it was obvious she wasn't that awake.

Mackenzie hesitated and stepped into the room.

"How'd it go?" Suzanne Brandt sat up in bed and gave a

two-fisted rub to her eyes. With her dark hair tousled and her face still flushed from sleep, she looked as innocent as the four-year-old she was helping to raise.

"They took it surprisingly well. If I didn't know better, I'd think they already had some idea it was coming."

"Well, do you think they finally figured out about Nick?"

Mackenzie sat down on her mother's bed. It had occurred to her that the Copelands might have already caught wind that she and Nick were husband and wife in name only, but when she had mentioned it to Nick, he had laughed it off.

"Nick seems to think that if they knew, they would have said something by now."

"Perhaps, but sometimes it's easier to just ignore things and hope they go away."

"I don't think they would have been so calm about it if they knew."

"What about your date? I'm assuming, since you are coming in so late, it went well?"

Mackenzie flushed. She and her mother had mended their fractured relationship when she became pregnant with Olivia. In her youth, Mackenzie had needed a mother she could talk to. Someone to take up for her when her father was calling her evil after finding her magazine cutouts of women taped to the inside of her closet door. Although Mackenzie had yet to fully let go of all the bitterness she associated with her last few years at home, she had gone straight to her mother when she got the news that she was pregnant. Her mother, to her shock, had reacted like a mother. She had taken Mackenzie in her arms and promised to be there for her and her child from then on. And she had.

Mackenzie stood. "I'm going to change before Olivia gets up and starts wondering why her mother is still wearing the same outfit she had on last night."

"It's a lovely dress."

Mackenzie smiled shyly at her mother's compliment and

smoothed the dress over her hips. "I felt good wearing it, right up until Barb said my arms looked too muscular."

"What did Colby think?"

Mackenzie smiled as she remembered the appreciative look Colby had given her. She would have suffered Barb Copeland's disproval a hundred times over just to have Colby look at her like that again. "I think she liked it a lot."

"Did you two talk?"

Mackenzie's smile faded a little. "I don't think she wants to talk about the past, and I can't risk..." Mackenzie shrugged. "I don't really know her, Mother. I want to, but it's not a good time. She lives in Portland and I live here. I have Olivia to think about. Women like Colby don't want kids in their lives."

"Are you sure about that? You said yourself you don't know her."

"I know enough to trust that if Colby wanted kids she would have them by now. She's smart. Driven." Mackenzie shrugged. "She always has been. Even if she was willing to try, I don't want Olivia to depend on her and then have Colby disappear from her life when we no longer fit into her lifestyle. Olivia's getting to the age where she's starting to realize it when people aren't there anymore. She's already asked me twice why Nick isn't living here."

"Are you worried about Olivia or yourself?"

Mackenzie leaned over, gave her mother a hug, and straightened to leave. "I'm worried about both of us."

❖

After Mackenzie left, Colby had lain in the bed for several minutes vacillating between wishing she'd had the guts to kiss Mackenzie good-bye and knowing why she hadn't. It was becoming too hard to keep it at just sex. If she had let Mackenzie know that she was awake, there would have been a conversation.

She would have had to tell the truth about why she was there and what she had been hired to do.

Colby slid from the bed flushing as sensitive places tingled, and she caught the scent of her own body and smiled. She wouldn't mind crawling back in bed and reliving last night's activities with Mackenzie. She picked up the letter and read it twice to make sure she had understood correctly.

Colby,

I'm sorry to have to leave like this, but I have to meet a client in two hours. Leaving you this morning was hard, which is one of the reasons I'm writing you this letter. I know I'm being a coward, but you are probably used to this kind of thing from me. I tried to explain it to you last night, but I had the feeling you didn't want to think about it. Unfortunately, it seems to be all I can think about. If we had met a year from now things might have been different, but I'm going through some messy things in my life. I know this was probably just a fun fling for you, but I'm afraid I can't afford to live my life like that.

I am so sorry for how I treated you in high school. I know that there is no excuse for it, but I was having a hard time at home with my sexuality, and you represented what I thought was wrong with me. I thought that by treating you cruelly it would make me stop wanting to know you. It only made it worse, and now I have that guilt to deal with too.

I know that you have a life in Portland, your business and other things that take precedence, but if things should ever change, or if you ever really want to talk about what happened to us back then, I'm here. I'm not running away.

Mackenzie

Colby tossed the note on the desk and walked into the bathroom to shower. That was it, then. Mackenzie had told her without saying it that she wouldn't see her anymore. Colby glanced at the damp towel neatly folded and hung on the towel rack and turned on the shower full blast. Halfway through lathering her body, Colby was calling Mackenzie all kinds of names that she wished she had thought of in high school. The realization that she was more hurt than angry calmed her. She had no right to be hurt. Mackenzie had simply done what she would have had to do if things had continued on the path they had been traveling.

Colby realized she had lost all objectivity. *If I ever had any in the first place, that is.* She shouldn't even be here. She had taken money to do a job and had slept with the married woman she was supposed to be proving was promiscuous. What did that say about her? Colby wrenched the knob to the off position, opened the door, and reached for a towel. The moment her hand touched its dampness, Colby realized it was the towel Mackenzie had used, but she pulled it into the shower anyway. Colby held it to her nose and closed her eyes. She didn't smell anything of Mackenzie. Just the same hotel soap she had just used. Colby dropped the towel outside the shower and pulled in a dry one. She roughly dried her body, her teeth gritted in determination. Mackenzie was right; this whole thing had been a mistake. It was time to be done with it.

CHAPTER SEVEN

Colby used the four-hour gap until her lunch meeting with the Copelands by checking her voicemail and e-mail, then working out in the hotel's fitness center. Even after a second shower, she still arrived at the hotel restaurant's outdoor patio twenty minutes before she expected to see the Copelands.

They were, of course, late. She would have been shocked if they had been on time. Her mind kept returning to the note. Mackenzie had very nicely—as nicely as someone can—dumped her.

"Ms. Dennis." Arnult Copeland was standing in front of her, and Colby rushed to greet him. His attention was already on the file folder, and Colby would not have been surprised if he had licked his lips. Colby had met many men like him. In her experience, as soon as they sensed blood in the water, they were quick to go in for the kill. In this case, that blood belonged to Mackenzie.

"Should we wait for Barb?" Colby asked.

"My wife had an important appointment she couldn't miss."

Colby narrowly kept from asking, "Hair, nails, or Botox?"

"Are those the photos?" Arnult asked and reached out to pick up the manila folder.

Colby stopped him with a hand on the file. She waited until

his sculpted gray eyebrows turned her way before she said, "We need to talk about what you hope to accomplish here, first."

"I'm sorry. I wasn't aware that we had anything else to talk about. You have your deposit. I can't imagine that didn't cover everything."

The change in Arnult Copeland's demeanor was slight, but Colby picked up on it instantly. *Slow down, Colby. Don't underestimate this man.* She leaned back and folded her arms, and as she suspected, Arnult Copeland removed his hand from the folder.

"I believe there are things you haven't told me. I'd like to know what those are before I turn over what I have."

Arnult's body went still. "Are you saying that you aren't going to give me the information I paid for?" Arnult's eyes had darkened to the color of coal. "I paid you to do a job, not think, Ms. Dennis."

Colby smiled and leaned forward. "You paid me—" She stopped speaking because Arnult's attention was now focused on something behind her. His face went slack with surprise. Colby frowned and turned around. Perhaps if she hadn't been so annoyed by Arnult's condescending tone she wouldn't have turned around so quickly and Nick Copeland might not have noticed that he had an audience. The moment he looked up, the smile on Nick's handsome, artificially tanned face faded. His gaze went from her to his father and back again. Nick leaned forward, said something to his equally attractive male companion, and stood. Despite the dread that descended over Colby as he approached, she couldn't help but analyze the man Mackenzie had married. Nick was handsome, if you went in for that rich playboy look. He walked with the assurance of someone used to getting attention. Nick's companion, a blond Adonis wearing a tank top and tight jeans, proved that point by watching with open curiosity as father and son shook hands like two business acquaintances.

"Dad, what are you doing here? Where's Mother?" Nick

looked her up and down twice. It made no difference that she was wearing one of her favorite tailored suits. Nick's gaze screamed "slut," and it both amused Colby and pissed her off.

"I'm having a meeting with a business associate," Arnult said as if Colby weren't sitting right there. "Your mother had an appointment with Dr. Polk. What are you doing here? Shouldn't you be at the office?"

"I'm having lunch with an old friend."

It hadn't escaped Colby's notice that the "old friend" still hadn't taken his eyes off Nick since he had walked over to their table. She also noticed that he looked an awful lot like Brad Pitt, if Brad Pitt was in the habit of drinking Bloody Marys with his pinky finger stuck out like he was having high tea with the Queen of England. Colby filed that bit of information away for later perusal.

"I'm sorry. We haven't been introduced. I'm Nick Copeland." Nick's gaze turned curious. "Have we met?"

Colby accepted his handshake, keeping her face friendly but blank. "Nice to meet you. I don't believe we have."

"Nick, Colby Dennis. Ms. Dennis, my son Nick."

Colby would have winced if Nick Copeland had not been standing right next to her. In general, she would have preferred that her real name not be put out there. It was obvious from Arnult's cavalier attitude that he either didn't care or didn't think his son capable of finding out his father was inserting his nose into his marital business. *Of course, who am I to judge? I've put more than just my nose in his marital business.* Colby did wince then.

"Why don't you come by the house later? Ms. Dennis is only in town for a few hours, and we have business to finish."

"Yes, of course," Nick said with the practiced air of a child used to being dismissed by a parent. "Ms. Dennis, it was nice meeting you."

Colby guessed by the way Nick's companion's face went

from happy to crestfallen that Nick had said something to curb his enthusiastic welcome back. *Why would the mere presence of his father in the restaurant ruin Nick Copeland's day?*

"Now, where were we?" Arnult asked.

"You were about to explain to me why these pictures are so important to you."

"Actually, I had no intention of explaining anything. You were hired to do a job. I've paid you for that job, which is all you are entitled to. Are we clear? You work for me. Not the other way around."

Colby nodded. "We are clear now." Colby slid the file across the table. With a glance toward Nick and his companion, Arnult opened the file and scowled at its contents. He picked up the first photo, the one of Mackenzie standing at the treadmill talking to Jessie with a far-off look on her face. Arnult lay that one face down and moved to the next. A photo of Mackenzie sitting in her office chair smiling at something. Colby liked that one the best because she had been the person Mackenzie was talking to, and it made her feel warm knowing that she could elicit such joy.

Arnult went through all twenty-eight innocuous photos, the confused look on his face deepening after each picture. "But none of these pictures show her with anyone."

"Because there was nothing to show."

"I don't understand. You found nothing? What is this?" Arnult held up his check.

"That, Mr. Copeland, is your retainer."

"I know what it *is*, I'm asking why it's here?"

"I'm returning it to you uncashed. I don't work for you. I work for myself."

"Do you know how many companies would bend over backward to get my business?"

Colby did know. She had hoped Arnult Copeland would take her photos and forget about his need to find dirt on Mackenzie. "I'm going to give you a little bit of unsolicited advice. Be careful who you hire to do this kind of work. Not everyone is as discreet as I am. Frankly, you seem to be taking this divorce a lot harder than your son." Colby looked toward Nick Copeland just in time to see him turn away and say something to his companion.

"Do you often return retainers when you don't find the information your client is looking for? You must have had expenses."

Colby shifted uncomfortably. In her effort to escape the guilt associated with taking Arnult's money, she had inadvertently shown her hand.

"Consider it a favor in deference to your friendship with Edward."

Arnult stared at her for several seconds before he nodded as if it made perfect sense that she would pay for her own hotel and expenses just because he went to school with one of her largest clients.

Colby stood with her hand out and Arnult did the same. "I'm sorry I couldn't give you what you were looking for."

"Well, you did your best." The comment was made coldly, the implication being that Colby had not done her best. Colby turned to walk out of the restaurant and almost as an afterthought looked toward Nick Copeland's table. It didn't surprise her that he would watch her so closely. He had just come upon his father having lunch with a younger woman in a hotel restaurant. The surprise came when she saw recognition cross his face just before she turned the corner. As she stood in front of the elevator that would eventually take her up to her room, she brooded over that look. Had he recognized her from the parking lot? By the time the elevator doors slid open, she was convinced she had imagined the look of recognition, and even if she hadn't, what difference did it make now?

❖

Mackenzie was closing Olivia's bedroom door when she saw Nick coming up the stairs with a worried look on his face.

She put her finger to her lips and pointed back down the stairs. If Olivia heard her father she would be up and out of bed in seconds. It had taken Mackenzie two stories and arm tickles to get her to go to sleep. If Nick woke her, he would be doing the honors of reading about Tidy Teddy Bear. Mackenzie had had her fill. Nick nodded, turned around, and took the stairs two at a time. Mackenzie followed at a slower pace. Something was wrong, but she wasn't in any hurry to find out what. She found Nick in the den pouring from the brandy decanter.

"You might want to let me fix one of these for you." Since neither of them were hardcore drinkers, Nick's going straight for the alcohol alerted Mackenzie to a serious problem. Not that she needed the glass in his hand to clue her in. Nick had gone from being her roommate to her best friend, husband, and finally, to being the father of her child. She could read him as easily as she read Olivia.

"What happened?"

"My parents. What else would drive me to drink?"

Mackenzie sat on the couch, took the glass Nick offered, and set it on the end table close enough to grab at a moment's notice.

"All right, tell me what they've done."

"I thought they were taking things so well. I just assumed that if they knew I was fine with it that they would leave well enough alone." Nick pushed back the lock of hair at his forehead, took a sip from his drink, and sighed. "I was having brunch at the Roheibeth Hotel with Seven…"

Mackenzie's tension eased. Now she understood Nick's apprehension. She had been uncomfortable seeing her mother after a night with Colby too. "Who's Seven?"

"His name is Mark. Seven is his number on our soccer team. He also looks just like Brad Pitt. He, uh, we've been seeing each other for a few weeks now."

"Is it serious?" Mackenzie raised her eyebrow. She and Nick had agreed that if either of them dated someone serious enough to bring around Olivia, they would introduce them to the other parent.

Nick shook his head, but he did blush, which meant that he thought things might go that way or he at least hoped they would. "We like each other a lot. I don't think he's any more into the game playing than I am. He knows all about my parents not knowing about me and he's cool with it, but that's not what I wanted to tell you. My father was there eating lunch with a woman."

"Do you think your father suspected anything, Nick? Were you two—"

"You don't understand. That's about the least of my worries. It's the woman he was with. When I came over to say hello, my father looked like he had been caught with his zipper down."

"Okay, so is that much of a surprise? You said yourself that you thought your parents each had their own dalliances."

"She went out of her way not to give me her name. Why do that unless she didn't want me to know who she was? My father was the one who said her last name. I Googled her. She's some kind of investigator in Portland."

Mackenzie frowned. "So what if she is? I'm sure your father has several reasons to hire an investigator."

"I saw her the other day outside the gym. She had something in her hand. I didn't see what it was before she slipped it in her pocket, but now I think…I think it might have been a camera."

It took several seconds for Mackenzie to process what Nick was hinting at. A woman was outside her window with a camera taking pictures of her at work. For what reason?

"Why would they hire someone to spy on me? That makes no sense. They already know about the divorce. We told them. What could they possibly have to gain?"

"I don't know, but I thought they took the news of the divorce too well."

Mackenzie nodded her agreement. "It was almost like they expected it."

Nick sat down next to her, reached across her, picked up her glass, and handed it to her. "You had a date the other night. Were you…discreet?"

Mackenzie swallowed. "As discreet as going to the Roheibeth hotel at ten at night can be. This is going to be messy, isn't it?"

Nick clenched his jaw. "You know I wouldn't let that happen," he said in a voice that Mackenzie almost found believable. But she had known Nick far longer than they had been married. His parents ruled his world. They were the reason she and Nick were even married. Mackenzie couldn't hate them completely. Without them, she might not have Olivia, but she had no misconceptions about the iron grip they had on Nick's life. Nick would never voluntarily tell them he was gay.

The severity of the situation struck home. If what Nick said was true, there had been a woman following her around with a camera. Taking pictures of her. Mackenzie stood. "I have to call Colby and warn her."

Nick stood and grabbed Mackenzie's wrist. "Colby? Colby Dennis? You know her?"

Mackenzie stopped. "Yes, she's the one I went to see at the hotel the other day. Before you get indignant about me not telling you, it wasn't serious and it's over. Nick, let go of me. I want to call her before it gets too late."

"She's the investigator."

"No, she owns her own sec—" Mackenzie felt her face go slack. "She said she owned a security firm."

"In Portland. She does. At least she didn't lie to you. Mackenzie? Mackenzie? Oh my God. Sit down."

Mackenzie allowed herself to be steered to the couch. What Nick was saying swam in and out of her head. Another mistake. Another bad decision. This time she had put Olivia in jeopardy, and that was unforgivable. She accepted the glass Nick handed her, and she must have drunk it because heat seared her throat.

Mackenzie would have cried if she could, but she was still too stunned. She flashed back to the shower, to the look of triumphant pleasure that had crossed Colby's face when she had gone down on her. The way she had brought her to orgasm more than once in the hotel room. The way Colby had taken her in the cab where anyone could have seen them. Mackenzie closed her lids over painfully dry eyes.

Nick's voice pushed its way into her consciousness. "Are you all right?"

Mackenzie nodded and looked at Nick's worried face. "You went out with her?" Mackenzie shook her head and Nick looked relieved. "Oh, thank God. For a minute there, I thought—"

Nick must have seen something in her face because he paled. "Please tell me you didn't have sex with her."

Chapter Eight

Dennis Security, Inc., Portland, Oregon

Two days after leaving Roheibeth, Colby slid the thin file into a storage box and sat back. It looked exactly like all the other boxes that sat untouched for years in the space she rented to keep her company files. This box, unlike the others, held something personal, something she had a role in screwing up, and she was having difficulty getting past that.

Colby reread the note, though she didn't need to. She practically knew the words by heart. She couldn't guess at the number of times she had intended to throw Mackenzie's note in the trash and had instead read it, folded it neatly, and placed it back in her briefcase. What was she saving it for? The note—Colby tried to think of it as what it really was, a brush-off letter—was simple. Mackenzie didn't want to see her anymore. She had known what little they had couldn't last, not when she had lied to Mackenzie from the very start. But she hadn't expected it to end so quickly.

"Asia, you busy?" The loud clack of Asia's keyboard silenced, and she heard her assistant push back from her desk. Asia appeared in the doorway with a frown on her normally pleasant face. "What's wrong?"

Asia shrugged. "You seem a little gruff today."

Colby tried to smile, but when Asia didn't bother to return her smile, she dropped the façade. "Yeah, sorry. I guess I'm just tired." *Damn right I'm tired. The last time I had a good night's sleep was at the Roheibeth Hotel with Mackenzie right before she snuck out like a criminal. Damn it, why can't I just let it go? Mackenzie doesn't owe me anything. She ended things before one of us got hurt. I respect her for doing what I couldn't.*

"Do you think you could have this box sent up to storage? I'd like to get it out of my office."

"Sure. I have some other stuff that needs to go up after lunch. I can take it all at once." Asia lifted the lid off the box and frowned at the nearly empty contents. "Oh, this is the Copeland case." She looked at Colby. "Is that what's bothering you? Are you worried that Edward is going to have a problem with how you handled everything?"

Colby rubbed the bridge of her nose. "I'm not worried about Edward. We've talked, and I explained that I did what I thought was right for the Copelands. Besides, the day I let one client determine how I do business with another is the day I pack it in. I'm just ready to get this out of my hair."

"All right." Asia picked up the box. "I'll just add the other file and take it up after lunch." She paused. "Hey, we're closed tomorrow. Maybe you should take advantage of the long weekend and take a vacation. I'll call you if something comes up."

Colby sighed. The truth was it had been a long time since she really needed to be in the office every day. Her people were hardworking and trustworthy. If there was an issue, Asia would make sure she knew about it. She continued to come in to work because she had nowhere else to go. Asia was halfway to the door before something she said clicked in Colby's head.

"What other file? That's the only one we have, isn't it?"

"I told you those background checks came in, remember?" Colby shook her head, and Asia frowned at her and continued to her desk. "I can't believe you don't remember. That's not like you. It's right here. I scanned it and there was nothing there."

"Still." Colby stood. "I'd like to see it just to make sure I…" *Just to make sure you did a thorough job of fucking up Mackenzie's life? Stop already.* "Asia, never mind. I…"

"Oh, here it is." Asia handed her the file before turning to answer the phone.

Colby quickly scanned each page of the report. She couldn't believe she had been too damn busy sleeping with the woman to remember the background report she had ordered. She wouldn't have guessed it in a thousand years, but it seemed that after Mackenzie was expelled from school she had taken her GED and then she had gone straight to the military. She'd only done four years before she seemed to drop off the face of the earth. Colby did the math in her head and decided that was when she had married Nick. Colby's eyes landed on a name and a date soon after Nick and Mackenzie married, and if not for the desk holding her up, she might have keeled forward. Olivia Marie Copland had been born exactly thirteen months after Nick and Mackenzie had been married. "She has a daughter?" *Why would she keep something like this a secret? Why would she tell you? You were just a fling to her.*

Asia ended her call and mistook Colby's shocked mutter as a question. "Yeah, look at this." Asia came around the desk and took the folder. She thumbed to the back and pulled out a photo. "Our guy says Mackenzie had this taken about three months ago. Isn't she cute?" Colby stared at the picture of the four-year-old. She had been used, but not by Mackenzie. There had always been something that reeked about the Copelands' story. She had never quite understood why they so desperately wanted the information they'd hired her to get. Now she thought she had the answer.

Colby took a deep, calming breath. She had given the Copelands nothing, but in the back of her mind she knew that someone like Arnult Copeland would not give up. Not without a fight.

❖

"All right, Joseph, I'm going to bump you up to the next level. Ready?" Mackenzie pushed the button on the treadmill and watched her client carefully to make sure he wasn't laboring more than she thought he should.

Mackenzie had been struggling not to look at the clock every five minutes. Normally, she avoided checking the time more than twice during a session because every client deserved her undivided attention. Keeping to that standard had proven difficult since Nick had dropped his bombshell about Colby.

Mackenzie glanced at the clock and was about to tell Joseph he had one more minute to go, but the words died in her throat. She had wondered if she would ever hear from Colby again. She'd never expected to see her again, and she certainly never expected to see her walking into her gym wearing a forest green sports bra and matching shorts. The woman hadn't an ounce of misplaced fat on her body. She was carrying a thick novel and a workout towel, but instead of hopping on one of the machines, Colby sat down in front as if waiting for an appointment. Mackenzie turned away from Joseph long enough to see Colby cross her legs and lean back in her chair. It had only been a few days since Mackenzie had last seen her, but when she stole a glimpse of her from the corner of her eye, it felt as if it had been years. Colby's hair fell forward with perfect symmetry as she scowled at the pages of her book. Mackenzie lingered on Colby's shoulders and trailed down to perfectly muscled legs. Runner's legs wouldn't look as nicely muscled as Colby's. Colby's shape had to have come from good old-fashioned squats and lunges. The thought brought a flash of arousal with it.

"Your next client?" Joseph asked as he loped along on the treadmill.

"Um, no. Come on, Joseph, you still have a way to go."

"It hasn't been twenty minutes yet?" The shocked look on his face would have been funny if Mackenzie didn't feel guilty about lying. Joseph had been one of her first clients. Over the last year, despite his insistence on drinking beer and eating pizza with his friends almost every weekend, he had lost thirty-six pounds. Mackenzie was constantly telling him that fat loss was eighty percent diet. But he was content with losing weight slowly. Joseph didn't know it yet, but his appointment had been over two minutes after Colby had walked though the door. Mackenzie was hoping Colby would get tired of waiting and just leave. She didn't want to talk to her. Confrontation wasn't her thing. Not anymore. There was something about Colby that brought out the worst in her. When she was younger she had dealt with these feelings by lashing out. Now she was afraid she might do something stupid—like cry.

Joseph looked at his watch and then slapped the red emergency stop button.

"What are you doing?" Panic made Mackenzie's voice climb. Colby looked up from her book. Mackenzie recognized the cover of a bestseller about witches living in modern-day Portland. She caught herself wondering if Colby still read thick paperback romances before pushing the thought away angrily. She didn't care what Colby read as long as she read it somewhere other than her gym.

"I've been on this torture mill for over thirty minutes. My titties can't take anymore. They need to make a sports bra for men."

Mackenzie glared at Joseph. "Stop calling them that. You don't have tit...breasts."

"My wife says they look better than hers." Joseph looked down at his chest. In his bent-over position, Mackenzie had to admit his chest did look like breasts. "I think she likes them like this," he said mournfully. Mackenzie blinked at Joseph for half a beat before a laugh escaped.

"Okay, time for you to go home."

"There it is, a real smile. I was starting to worry about you."

Joseph sighed. "You want me to stay while you…" He gave a slight nod toward Colby.

Mackenzie looked at Colby and back at Joseph. "I'll be fine. You are very observant for a guy. Was I that obvious?"

"Nah, it's the titties. They give me special powers."

Mackenzie mock punched Joseph's shoulder. She thought she saw Colby look up, but when she looked toward her she was still looking at her book. Her scowl had gone from mild to ferocious, though.

"Okay, thanks for the workout," Joseph said and picked up his towel. With dread, Mackenzie remembered that since Joseph went straight home after his workouts, he didn't stop off in the locker room. In seconds, she and Colby were alone. Mackenzie waited for Colby to look up from her book. When she didn't, Mackenzie busied herself racking the weights and placing the exercise bands and balls in their proper places. She wiped down the equipment slowly and kept one eye on Colby, who seemed to be so engrossed in her book that Mackenzie almost dared to hope she could walk right by her and Colby wouldn't even look up.

Finally, Mackenzie turned off the music. Colby closed her book and looked up. Her face was so composed that an unexpected yet not unfamiliar anger flared in Mackenzie's chest. Mackenzie began the mental relaxation techniques she had begun to rely on to keep her temper in check. She forced her shoulders to relax, then her hands and jaws. All of which was hard to do when Colby was looking at her so strangely.

"I'm a little outside of your neighborhood, aren't I?" Mechanize asked, managing to keep the sarcasm out of her voice.

"A little, but I've heard great things, and I need a personal trainer."

"We're closed and I don't have any openings."

Colby nodded, calmly stood, book in hand, and walked toward the front door.

Mackenzie felt her mouth hang open and clamped it shut right before Colby turned around, hand on the front door. "I'll see you tomorrow."

"Wait. What? What do you mean you'll see me tomorrow?"

"I mean, I'll be back tomorrow, and the next day, and the next if I have to."

"That's Sunday. I'm closed on Sunday."

"Then I'll come back on Monday."

"For what? Haven't you done enough?" Anger was hot in Mackenzie's chest, and there would be no willing it away. Not this time.

"So you know." It was a statement, not a question.

"That you're a liar? Yeah, I know."

"I never lied to you," Colby said vehemently.

"When did you tell me the truth? You came to the reunion to seduce me so that you could get proof for Arnult and Barb."

"I did not."

Mackenzie wanted to scream at her to leave, to get out of her life so she could start cleaning up what was left of it. But she was clenching her jaw so tightly that no words came out. Colby stopped just short of touching her. She was standing so close Mackenzie had to look down. The mistake was looking in her eyes. How could Colby still look so innocent after what she had done?

"I didn't know what they wanted, Mackenzie. They told me you were cheating on Nick, so I thought—"

"So you thought it would be perfectly acceptable to have sex with me in the locker room?"

"I didn't plan that part, Mackenzie. You might never believe anything else I tell you, but you have to believe that."

Mackenzie turned away from Colby's beseeching gaze. That was just it. She didn't have to believe a word Colby said. But looking at Colby made her think of high school and of how her inability to communicate made her feel so helpless she lashed out. She was proud of who she had become and hated the person she used to be. She wouldn't let Colby Dennis turn her into that person again.

"Why are you here, Colby?" The quicker she got this over, the sooner she could move on with her life.

"I'm here…I'm here to tell you how sorry I am."

"Sorry doesn't quite cover what you did."

"What did I do, Mackenzie? Tell me what you think I did, because I think we're talking about two different things and I need to understand what I'm defending myself against." Colby's face was flushed with frustration. Even now, as angry as she was, Mackenzie was finding it next to impossible not to stare at Colby's chest.

"They lied to me. They never told me about Olivia. They only told me half the truth."

"And you, in turn, told *me* half of that truth. In my book, that makes you a liar too."

Colby couldn't have looked more stunned if Mackenzie had reached out and slapped her. "You're right. I can't deny it, but *you* neglected to tell *me* you have a daughter."

Mackenzie momentarily forgot what they were arguing about. She wasn't sorry she hadn't told Colby about Olivia. Her loyalty was to her daughter. Her job was to protect Olivia. Colby was a fling, something to be kept far away from Olivia. If their affair had continued, she expected that Colby would have ended things anyway. What she didn't expect was the hurt look on Colby's face. That look siphoned some of the steam off her anger and left confusion in its place.

"Will you just talk with me about this? Please?" Colby asked.

"There's nothing to talk about. You were hired to do a job. You did it." Mackenzie turned to walk toward her office. She had hoped that Colby would take the hint and leave. When Colby followed her instead, the anger she had worked so hard to curtail burst to the surface. She turned around with a hand out.

"Enough, damn it." She hadn't expected her to be so close. Her hand hit Colby's chest with a thunk that stopped Mackenzie's heart.

The shocked look on Colby's face crumpled Mackenzie's resolve. "Oh, my God, Colby! I didn't mean to do that." She pulled Colby close, her heart breaking as she realized how much smaller Colby was. When Colby relaxed, Mackenzie pushed the anger and the questions from her mind. *Just for a minute. Just for a minute.*

"Mackenzie, just give me a chance to make this better. Afterward, if you still want me to go, I will. I promise I won't ever…" Colby paused, and something in that pause made Mackenzie hope for things that made her feel foolish and raw. "I won't ever come back." Colby finished as if the words had been dragged out of her.

For several long moments, Mackenzie was able to hold her tears at bay by focusing her anger at Colby, at her in-laws, and to a lesser degree, at Nick for not being able to stand up to them. But soon anger was not enough, and the dam opened without warning.

Mackenzie wilted and Colby, with the help of the gym mirrors, held her up. Mackenzie recognized the gentle shushing sound coming from Colby. She had used it on Olivia enough times to know that it was more habit than anything. Colby's hand was between her and the mirror rubbing her back and coaxing the sobs out of her. Mackenzie rested her head on Colby's shoulder. She wasn't a pretty crier. She shouldn't be letting Colby hold her like this, but it had been so damn long since anyone had.

"I am so very sorry for my part in all this," Colby said in a near whisper after Mackenzie's sobs had quieted.

Mackenzie straightened and spent a few seconds avoiding Colby's eyes. Colby's hands on her face forced her to meet Colby's gaze. She knew her face would be splotchy and her nose swollen, not to mention the snot threatening to come from her nostrils, but Colby's gaze never wavered, and for the first time

Mackenzie noticed Colby's damp cheeks. Colby was trying hard to get her to meet her gaze, but Mackenzie steeled herself against the sincerity she glimpsed in Colby. She couldn't afford to see it or believe it. Not now. Not ever again.

"You can't possibly understand the magnitude of what you did. Whatever info you gave them, they will use it to run me into the ground. I can't afford the lawyers that they can."

"What about Nick? I know you're getting a divorce. Is it because he found out about you?"

"He's known all along. I never lied to Nick. We were married in name only. My father wanted proof that I wasn't a lesbian, and his parents wanted him to have the house, the kids, and the white picket fence. We thought we could make our parents happy by adding a piece of paper. We figured, why not? We're already roommates. We fooled ourselves into thinking nothing would change, but we would give ourselves a pretty life to hide in. We were idiots."

"Why doesn't he just tell his parents that he knows you're a lesbian and he's fine with how you're raising Olivia?"

"Because we have an agreement. I can't change the rules now."

"He's gay, isn't he?"

Mackenzie hesitated.

"It's okay. You don't have to answer. I already know he is. But Olivia *is* Nick's biological daughter, right? Please don't take this the wrong way. The Copelands can't expect him to fight you for custody if you two went to the sperm bank."

"Olivia is Nick's daughter," Mackenzie said defensively, and the flash of disappointment on Colby's face was so quick she thought she had imagined it. "We did it the old-fashioned way."

"Okay." Colby released her and backed away.

Mackenzie felt the drop in body heat when Colby's body was no longer pressed into hers. Colby wrapped her arms around herself and looked down. Words tumbled out of Mackenzie's mouth. "Turkey baster," she said and then flushed.

"You and Nick with a...?" Colby looked pleased then confused and then pleased again. "So you didn't...?"

"No." Mackenzie loved Nick, but the idea of actually consummating their marriage had only occurred to either of them once, and that had left them both queasy and in search of alcohol.

"Yes, we used Nick's sperm, but my friend Palmer helped me. Olivia is most definitely both Nick's and my flesh and blood."

Colby spoke slowly as if searching for the correct words. "Is Palmer your lover?"

Mackenzie took a deep breath. "How could you even ask me that? I know this might be hard for you to believe after what Arnult and Barb may have told you and what we did at the reunion, but I do not sleep around." Mackenzie bit the last few words out like bullets.

"I'm sorry. I believe you. I just needed to know for sure."

"Then you probably should have asked a long time ago. And another thing, if I did have a lover, I certainly would not have had sex with you!" Mackenzie stifled a sob and continued angrily in the hopes that one emotion would overcome the other. "I am not a slut and I am..." Colby was holding her again, and it was hard for her to get the rest out, but she did, just to hear it said out loud because if the Copelands had their way, she wouldn't be hearing herself described that way anytime soon. "I am a damn good mother."

❖

"What do you have for me, Asia?" Colby said brusquely into the phone. The coffee and meager breakfast she had forced down her throat had done nothing to quell the turmoil in her stomach.

"Well, hello to you too. I've had a fine day despite a phone call at the ass crack of dawn from my boss. Thanks for asking."

Colby barely kept from snapping. "Look, I screwed up. Mackenzie Brandt-Copeland was—is a friend of mine. Her in-laws were out to hurt her, and I let old baggage between us get in the way of my better judgment. I need to help her, and I guess it's making me crazy. I'm really sorry for snapping at you."

Asia was silent for a long time. "You've never apologized to me before."

"Really?" Colby frowned. "Well, I'm sorry for that too."

Asia cleared her throat. "Anyway, I was just calling to tell you that the people I have gotten to call me back don't seem to be dealing with the Copelands. I'll keep trying, but why do you think they hired someone else after you closed the case?"

"Arnult Copeland doesn't give up."

"All right, I'll keep trying. But a lot of these places aren't too forthcoming about their client list. They think we're poaching."

"I appreciate you're doing all of this. Oh, and, Asia, I know you'll get paid overtime, but I still want you to schedule paid time off after this is over with. I'm sure that new boyfriend isn't happy about you having to work on your day off."

"Are you all right? I mean really all right?"

Colby had to laugh at Asia's suspicious tone. "To be honest, I feel like a piece of crap. But I'm working on feeling better about myself, and you're helping me. So you'll keep at this?"

Asia assured her that she would and Colby hung up the phone and sat down at the small hotel desk. She was faced with a night of either pretending to read the book she had purchased at the gas station or trying to sleep. She wasn't even sure what she was doing there. Mackenzie had made it clear that she blamed Colby for at least some of what was happening to her. *But she did let you hold her, and she didn't react when you said you would call her. That means something...doesn't it?* It meant Mackenzie was scared. It meant she was willing to accept any help she could get. It meant she was desperate and nothing more. Colby stood just as her cell phone rang. She picked it up and almost didn't answer when she didn't recognize the phone number. At the last minute she pressed the green phone button.

"Hi, it's Mackenzie. Your assistant gave me your phone number."

"That's fine, I'm glad she did." Colby sat on the bed. Just hearing Mackenzie made her feel better. "How are you doing?"

"A little embarrassed. I'm sorry for breaking down like that. It's the waiting that's killing me. I feel like I should just go over there and knock some sense into them, but they haven't done anything."

They haven't done anything yet, Colby thought.

"I keep hoping Nick is right and they are just taking precautions to protect the family money. I decided it was time to stop waiting for them to make the first move. They've agreed to have dinner at the house on Monday. I was hoping we could get this out in the open."

Colby scowled at nothing. "Do you think that's a good idea?"

"I'm not sure, but I need to know what they intend to do with the information they wanted from you."

"Mackenzie, I know you don't believe me, but there was nothing in the pictures I gave them that could hurt or embarrass you. In fact, I told them to leave it alone."

"Do you think they listened?"

"Honestly, no. I don't."

Mackenzie sighed. "I don't think so either. I can't imagine what they hope to gain from any of this other than to embarrass me around town. It's not as if any court is going to take my child away from me just because I'm a lesbian."

Colby had been wondering the exact same thing. "I obviously don't know them half as well as you do, but there has to be some angle that we aren't seeing."

"This waiting around is killing me."

"How would you feel about me being at your dinner? I know it's a family thing, but they sort of got me involved."

"You'd be willing to do that?"

"Absolutely. Monday night, right?"

"Yes. Unfortunately, they're at the coast for the Fourth of July, or I'd try to meet with them sooner."

Colby realized she had forgotten there was even a holiday coming up. "Listen, do you think you could set up a meeting between Nick and me? I'd like to speak with him before his parents try to influence him."

"You don't have to do all this, you know. I believe you about not knowing what they intended. This isn't your fight."

Colby couldn't keep her words from wavering. "I need to do this."

"Colby, I have to be honest. I can't continue the way things were. That's exactly what the Copelands are looking for. I have to think about Olivia now. I'm sorry."

"I understand," Colby said around the lump in her throat. She hadn't realized that she was holding on to hope until Mackenzie told her in so many words that there was none.

"She means everything to me. She's my world."

"Okay." The awkwardness was tangible through the phone.

Finally, Mackenzie sighed. "I'm meeting Nick tomorrow at Kensington Park. Do you know where that is?"

Colby knew the place. Kensington Park was where the popular kids used to hang upside down on monkey bars while smoking cigarettes halfway to the filter before dropping them in the sand for elementary school kids to find later. Colby had never hung out there, though she had secretly yearned to.

"I know where it is. What time and what's the occasion?"

"Ten o'clock. Nick has Olivia over the long holiday weekend. We usually like to meet in the park so it doesn't bring up the inevitable questions of why he doesn't live with us anymore."

"Oh." Colby flushed. Olivia would be there. Why did the possibility of meeting Mackenzie's daughter bother her more than seeing Nick Copeland? "Don't take this the wrong way, but do you trust Nick with Olivia? You don't think the Copelands would try to take her while she's with him?"

"No, I don't. I've already told Nick I don't want them around her, and he's agreed not to go over there. I couldn't forbid him to see her even if I wanted to. He's her daddy and she loves him."

Colby sighed. "Okay, but if you think there might be a danger, there are things we can do, even if it's only temporary."

"I've thought about that, but there's no point antagonizing them before they even show their hand."

"I agree. Okay, so I'll meet you at the park. Ten a.m." Colby said, "Good-bye," and hung up. She could have easily been talking to any number of clients for the formality of the conversation. Mackenzie had said it was over between them. *Come on, Colby, what did you expect? It's not as if 2.5 fucks constitute a relationship.* Colby pulled three bottles from the mini-bar and set them on the desk.

Five bucks for a miniscule bottle of gin? It's a good thing I'm not much of a drinker, or I'd go broke.

The first bottle would get her tipsy. If she was lucky, the other two would leave her comfortably comatose.

CHAPTER NINE

Kensington Park, 9:50 Friday morning

Mackenzie had the petty and unsympathetic thought that Colby must have had a worse night than she had. Her pleasure soon faded when she realized that Colby, unlike her, might not have gone to bed at nine p.m. For all Mackenzie knew, Colby might owe her weary appearance to having met someone at Panda's, the only gay club between Roheibeth and Portland.

Palmer had dragged Mackenzie to Panda's on several occasions. She'd said it was to remind her that she was still a lesbian. Mackenzie had to admit she would sometimes go weeks without yearning for the company of another woman. As Colby drew closer, Mackenzie wondered when she would stop thinking about how good it felt to touch her, kiss her lips, and run her hands through her hair.

"Hi." Colby handed her a cup of coffee and several small white, pink, and blue packets. "I bought coffee. I wasn't sure if you took sweetener or cream."

Mackenzie shook her head, still unable to look at Colby directly for fear she would see what she had been thinking. "Thank you. I didn't realize it would be so chilly out here or I would have stopped and bought some myself. And this is perfect. I take my coffee black." Mackenzie sipped coffee and scooted over as, to her surprise, Colby stepped up on the bench and joined her in sitting on the table. The higher perch gave Mackenzie a better view of the slide.

A squeal drew Mackenzie's attention to where her daughter followed an older little boy up the ladder.

Olivia, unlike her, had never had trouble meeting new people. The child was so gregarious that Mackenzie had to sit her down and give her "the stranger talk" several times to remind her that not everyone deserved a hug. It had almost broken her heart when Olivia had reacted as if she were being chastised, but Mackenzie did what she had to do to protect her child. Finally, she looked at Colby. She'd do anything for Olivia, and that included forgetting about any pain Colby had caused her.

"I'm sorry I lost control yesterday."

"You're handling it better than most would. Is Nick still coming?"

"Of course he is. Don't you think I would have called you if he had canceled?" Mackenzie realized that she sounded much sharper than she'd meant to. "I'm sorry."

Colby nodded, watching as Olivia slid down the slide, this time with her hands up like the older boy was doing. "She's beautiful."

"Yes."

"She's four, right?"

"Almost. Her birthday is next month. Seems like I just brought her home from the hospital yesterday. I had this irrational fear I was going to drop her, so for the longest time I would sit down every time I held her."

Colby smiled. "You got over that, huh?"

"Had to. Couldn't sit down every time I needed to hold her. My mother helped a lot. She still does." Mackenzie smiled as she thought of her mother. Olivia doted on her grandmother, and if she weren't so appreciative of the care her mother showed Olivia, she would be jealous.

As if she had read her mind, Colby asked, "You two close?"

"We are now. She stays with me and looks after Olivia while I'm working."

"Are your parents still married?"

Mackenzie tried to keep her smile in place, but it slipped anyway. This was just small talk, the kind of thing anyone would ask, but it brought back memories she would rather not have thought about. "My parents split up right before Olivia was born. My mother moved in with me after I had Olivia, but my dad..." Mackenzie shrugged. "He felt I took my mother's side of things. I haven't heard from him since. I don't even know where he is."

Colby's face paled visibly. "Oh, I am so sorry. I had no idea."

"It's okay. We weren't that close." Mackenzie's mind rebelled the moment she let the words slip past her lips. It was true, they hadn't been close for years, but things had been better between them after she had married Nick. She had been Daddy's little girl. He'd brought her to this very park when she was small. He had been the loudest in the crowd at every one of her sports events. He had been there for her.

Right up until she turned fifteen.

"How about your parents? They moved out of town, didn't they?" Her question was an obvious attempt at changing the subject, but if Colby noticed, she didn't let on.

"My parents were hippies living out of a station wagon in Colby Woods until I was born and they had to go mainstream."

"Um, Colby Woods?"

"You want to hear this story or not?"

Mackenzie made a choking sound and apologized.

"Anyway, a week after I graduated and left for college, they sold the house here and bought one of those big Winnebago things and never looked back."

"That sounds like fun. Do you ever get to see them?"

"Oh yeah. They stopped in Portland last summer to see my office. They camped out in the parking lot of my office building for a week."

"You're kidding?"

"I'm not." Colby was laughing, but Mackenzie heard the ire in her laugh. "They set up a grill in the handicapped spot. They figured that as long as it was after five, no one should complain since all sensible folks and the handicapped are at home by that time anyway. The other tenants in my office park still look at me funny."

"Do you miss them?"

Colby sobered. "Sometimes. When I was young they used to embarrass me."

"And now?" Mackenzie asked.

Colby looked at Mackenzie. "Now I envy them their ability to be so carefree. I've never been like that. Well, almost never." Colby looked down at the bench between her feet, and Mackenzie wondered if she was thinking about the reunion.

"That was one of the first things I noticed about you. You were always so serious."

"Not always."

Mackenzie smiled. "Pretty much."

"And you know this because of how close we were in high school?"

Mackenzie's smile slipped. "I noticed things about you even back then. You used to walk around with your books held tight to your chest as if you thought someone was going to come along and do something to you."

"You mean do something like steal my favorite books and throw them in the trash?" Colby asked gently.

Mackenzie dipped her head. She had been angry at Colby for being involved with the Copelands, but Colby still had good reasons to be angry with her too. She *had* taken her books, and she *had* thrown them in the trash, but not before she read them. "That's not what I meant. I always thought you looked afraid. And I don't mean of me. I mean of the world. Like if you took one wrong step things could go bad and you would come unmoored. The reason I recognized it, or at least I thought I did, was because I always felt that way too." Mackenzie looked up to see if Colby was listening, but Colby was looking toward the slide with a frown on her face. Mackenzie surmised that Colby had seen Olivia being pushed down by her taller friend. Colby stood on the park bench as if she was about to call out.

Mackenzie touched her arm gently to restrain her. "Wait. Just watch."

Colby turned her frown on Mackenzie and then back to the kids. "He's bigger than she is. He shouldn't be—"

"I know, but she can handle herself." Almost as if she had heard her mother, Olivia stood. She put her finger in her playmate's face, and with a hand on her hip, said something that Colby couldn't hear. She stomped away and started climbing the ladder. The dumbstruck look on Colby's face was mirrored on the face of Olivia's playmate.

"What did she say?"

"She said real men don't hit womens," Mackenzie said solemnly.

"Womens?"

"She saw it on *Popeye*."

Colby nodded and returned to her seat atop the picnic table. "Makes perfect sense."

"And if that doesn't work, she has a mean uppercut." Colby was staring at the side of her face, waiting for her to look at her. Mackenzie took her time sipping her coffee.

"If someone had told me ten years ago you would become a mother I would have laughed them out of town."

Mackenzie swallowed carefully so as not to burn her throat before responding. "And now?"

"Now, I can't imagine why I was so surprised when I found out." Mackenzie heard the change in Colby's voice, but she acted as if she didn't. "Oh, no…um, she's coming over." Colby looked as if she was going to stand up.

"Just sit still, she won't bite," Mackenzie said softly. "Haven't you ever been around kids before?"

"Not outside the grocery store."

"Oh, that's a good start."

"You're laughing at me," Colby said stiffly.

"I am, and I like it much better than crying on your shoulder."

"I do too."

Mackenzie leaned down and wrapped her arms around her legs just as Olivia reached the table. "Hi, Mama."

"Hey, Lil Bird, you cold?"

"No, but I'm smoking. See?" Olivia blew a white fog out of her mouth.

"Smoking's not healthy."

"Popeye smokes a pipe."

"Popeye also eats spinach and asparagus. You planning on giving those a shot too?"

"No." Mackenzie reached out an arm and Olivia grabbed on to it. She pulled her up and sat her on the table between herself and Colby.

"Then I'm thinking you should forget about the smoking until your thirty-seventh birthday. We can revisit this discussion then." She paused and winked at Colby over Olivia's head. "Olivia, this is my friend Colby. We went to school together."

"Hello, Olivia." Colby looked as if she was going to stick her hand out but put it in her pocket instead.

"Hi. Do you smoke?"

Colby looked at Mackenzie for help, but Mackenzie looked as if she was interested in the answer. "No, I mean sometimes when I have a dri—when I'm out with friends I'll—not often."

"You should stop. My mama doesn't like it."

"Okay. In that case, I'll never do it again."

Olivia patted Colby's leg and said, "Good girl." Colby

smiled triumphantly, and Mackenzie almost choked in her effort not to laugh.

"Daddy!" Olivia shouted, jumped up, and would have leaped off the bench if Mackenzie hadn't caught her with a one-handed grab and lowered her to the ground. She streaked across the park and was scooped up in the arms of her father.

"Popeye ate asparagus?" Colby asked.

"No, but I wanted to put it out there just in case she was willing to negotiate."

Colby chuckled as Nick tossed Olivia in the air. The look on his face left no doubt in her mind that he loved his little girl. "I can see both of you in her."

"I think she looks more like me."

"Yeah, maybe. She seemed to like me."

Mackenzie turned to tell Colby that kids, especially her kid, rarely disliked people on sight, but Colby's face was so heartbreakingly serious that Mackenzie was reminded of the young, lonely girl who had always been on the outskirts of everything. Colby might look different now, but there was still so much of her that was the same. Mackenzie spoke without thought. "How could anyone not like you, Colby?"

Colby seemed to struggle to find the right words. "Lots of people don't."

"Is that why you hide who you really are?"

"Well, this is a surprise."

Mackenzie tore her eyes away from Colby to look at Nick. Luckily, Nick had slung Olivia over his shoulder as he approached so she would be unaware of the ferocious frown he was wearing as he looked from Colby to Mackenzie.

"What are you doing here?" Nick jostled Olivia a little and pretended to let her go over the back of his shoulder.

She let out a breathless, "No, Daddy," and dissolved into giggles.

"Nick, don't you ever check your voicemail? I left you a message explaining that I had invited Colby along."

Nick looked sheepish for an instant, but that faded into another scowl. Again, he spoke to Colby. "How much are my parents paying you to spy on us?"

"Colby, don't answer that."

"It's all right, I don't mind answering. First of all, your parents didn't ask me to spy on"—Colby made quotes in the air with her fingers before she said added a snarky—"*us*. They asked me to investigate Mackenzie. If I *had* taken their money, my fees would be none of your da—none of your business." Colby looked directly at Mackenzie. "I returned their check." Mackenzie broke eye contact with her first. "Now your turn."

Nick raised an eyebrow. "What do you mean, my turn?"

"Your parents are out to cause trouble for Mackenzie," Colby said carefully. "I want to know what you're going to do about it."

Mackenzie's heart lurched at the thought the Copelands could possibly take it that far.

"That's ridiculous. This is all a misunderstanding. Either way, why should I discuss any of this with you? I don't even know you."

"Fine, don't tell me. Tell your daughter's mother. I'm sure she'd like to know the answer."

Mackenzie had rarely seen Nick so angry. She was glad Olivia seemed content to rest on his shoulder for the time being. "Fine. I'd say she's my daughter's mother and a damn fine one. I'd also say she's my best friend and I don't, for a moment, regret marrying her. But that we aren't suited for each other in that capacity."

Colby nodded. "That's good to hear. Just one more question. Are you so afraid of your parents that you are willing to put your 'best friend' and 'your daughter's mother' through hell just to hide your sexuality from them? Do you really think they don't already know?"

Nick seemed at a loss for words. "Mackenzie, may I speak with you for a second?"

"Um, yeah, why don't you walk me to my car to get Olivia's bag?" Mackenzie looked at Colby. She was surprised by the level of anger coming from Colby. "I'll be back, all right?"

Colby barely nodded. And Mackenzie walked off with Nick feeling as if she had done something wrong.

"Did you tell her?" he asked stiffly when they had walked out of earshot.

"She's not an idiot, Nick. She saw you at the hotel with your friend. By the way, if she could guess so easily, I have no doubt what she said is right. I think they know. I think they've known for a long time."

Nick looked annoyed. "If they knew, why wouldn't they say anything?"

"That's something you'll have to ask them when all this finally comes out."

"Don't trust her, Mackenzie. She's just graduated from peeping into your window to trying to be your friend."

"Nick, I know this is hard for you to believe, but I am capable of making decisions for myself."

"I understand that, but my parents aren't just anyone. When they get it in their heads that they're right about the outcome of something—"

"Then do something about it, Nick. For fuck's sake!"

"Ooh, you cursed," Olivia murmured in a hushed whisper from her position on Nick's shoulder.

Nick rolled his eyes as if *he* had never slipped. "Mackenzie, I've already told them you're a good mother and that our divorce is completely amicable. What else can I tell them?"

"How about you start with the truth about your sexuality, our marriage, and finish with the fact that they were awful parents who tried to pay other people to make you happy your whole life?"

Nick paled. "I can't do that."

"Then don't question me about Colby's motives, Nick. She's trying to help, which is more than I can say for you."

Mackenzie opened the door of her SUV and handed Olivia's bag to Nick. She looked toward the park bench where Colby still sat. Whether it was to give them privacy or just a change in position, Colby had shifted so that her back was to the trio.

"You know I would do anything I could to help, but I just can't do that."

Mackenzie wanted to say, *Then you wouldn't do anything*, but she, of all people, knew what it felt like to try to earn a parent's love by pretending to be someone she wasn't. Even though she didn't have any reason to lie anymore. Nick had been there when no one else had.

"Then just let it go. I've decided to trust her. I've asked her to have dinner with us on Monday. Your parents won't have any reason not to put things out on the table if they see her there."

"You're still sleeping with her, aren't you?"

"No, that part of our relationship is over." Mackenzie sighed. "But she still wants to help, and at this point I'm willing to accept whatever help I can get."

Nick was about to say something else, but Olivia was getting cranky and insisted she be put down. Mackenzie bent down, kissed her, and told her to be good for her father. She waited while Nick fastened Olivia into her car seat. Mackenzie waved at her through the window. "Call me if she has nightmares, and watch to make sure she doesn't get scared during the louder fireworks."

"I will. Just promise me you'll be careful around that woman, okay?"

Mackenzie nodded, and with one last wave to Olivia, she started back toward the picnic table and Colby's hunched form. The wind had picked up, and just as she sometimes did with Olivia, she wondered if Colby's light jacket was protection enough. Mackenzie felt an odd twinge after thinking something so sentimental about the woman she had been having sex with, but Colby looked so damn small sitting there like that.

Mackenzie sat next to Colby, but before she could utter a word she realized Colby had fallen asleep with her elbows propped on her knees and her cheeks between her hands. At first Mackenzie looked away, feeling guilty about catching Colby so unawares. After several minutes of waiting for Colby to wake up, she began to steal surreptitious glances at Colby until finally, she was openly staring. She had always loved the way Colby's lips were shaped. They were so full and soft looking. Kissing them made her want to hum with pleasure.

Mackenzie was still staring at Colby's mouth when she opened her eyes. The heat of attraction flared between them. Mackenzie leaned forward, drawn by the passionate demand in Colby's eyes, only to see it disappear as quickly as it had appeared.

"I fell asleep, didn't I?" Colby said in an obvious attempt to break the tension.

"Yeah, sorry. I didn't want to wake you. You looked exhausted. Long night?"

Colby chuckled. "Yeah. The air conditioner in my room ticked all night. I couldn't get the damn thing to turn off."

"Why didn't you ask them to fix it?"

"It was late when I realized it was a problem. Tonight won't be much different. I was told the handyman was out sick and there are no other rooms available."

"I have an extra room."

Colby opened her mouth and then closed it. "That's very generous of you, but don't you think that's a bad idea?"

"It would be if my mother's room wasn't next to mine."

Colby's eyes widened, and she shivered.

"Makes me shiver too. I think we're safe. Come on." Mackenzie stood. "You can just follow me home."

"Mackenzie? You acted as if you didn't believe me before and now you're letting me stay in your home. Are you sure you want to do this? I can make them call someone out to fix the air conditioner or even stay in a hotel outside of town."

"I'd like you to stay with me if you're comfortable with it."

"Okay, thank you. I accept your offer."

"Good." Mackenzie smiled. "Now hurry up before it starts raining. We'll swing by the hotel so you can check out." Mackenzie took advantage of having a longer stride, keeping far enough ahead of Colby that she wouldn't see her face. Her offer of a room had been genuine. Her instant burst of pleasure when Colby accepted almost made her want to rescind the offer. Why was she so worried? It wasn't like this was one of those romance novels Colby used to read in high school. They were adults. She wasn't quite ready to call them friends, but she didn't think Colby thought of her as an enemy anymore. They could spend time together without having sex with each other. Then, in the span of a second, Mackenzie peeked at Colby from the corner of her eye, decided she loved Colby in jeans, thought about dropping back slightly in the hopes of seeing Colby's ass, and realized she was screwed.

❖

Colby didn't know what she had been thinking accepting Mackenzie's offer to stay with her. A better question might have been what had Mackenzie been thinking offering her the room in the first place? It wasn't as if they were friends. As true as that statement was, thinking it made Colby feel sad. She pulled into the driveway and parked next to Mackenzie's SUV.

She tried to read Mackenzie's face as she got out of the car, but there was absolutely nothing there and it worried her. "Are you sure about this? If it's going to make you uncomfortable, I can go back to the hotel and check back in."

Mackenzie looked at her, as if only just realizing Colby was standing there. "Why would you do that?"

"I don't know. You looked like you were upset. I just wanted to make sure you weren't regretting your offer."

"I was wondering if Olivia would be okay with the fireworks tomorrow. She tries to act brave, but loud noises scare her and Nick isn't the most observant person in the world."

Colby flushed. Of course she was missing her daughter. *Everything isn't about you, idiot.*

"Maybe you could call him and remind him."

"No, he's going to need to get used to taking care of her on his own. I just…"

"You just worry about your little girl. There's nothing wrong with that. I think it's…" Colby searched for the right word. "I think it's good that kids know there's someone who worries about them. It makes them feel…"

"Safe?"

"Yeah, I guess." Colby dipped her head under the pretense of taking her bag out of the passenger's seat of her car. Why hadn't she kept her damn mouth shut?

It had only been seconds since they had spoken, but Colby felt discomfiture settle over her. She wondered how she was going to spend the evening with a woman she could barely even look at. The front door swung open, and if Colby's foot hadn't already been up she would have probably tripped over the step. Mackenzie's mother—and it couldn't be anyone else but Mackenzie's mother—was standing in the doorway. A surprised look came over her face as she spotted Colby behind Mackenzie. She smiled and Colby was treated to a vision of Mackenzie twenty years later. She felt her face heat up. It was official; she was a damn heathen.

"Colby Dennis, isn't it?" Colby flushed again and stepped up on the porch with her hand out. But Mackenzie's mom pulled her into an embrace so warm Colby was almost too shocked to return it. She clumsily patted the woman's back and then stepped back.

"Hello, Ms. Brandt, it's really nice to meet you."

"You should call me Suzanne. Mackenzie has spoken of you often. Come on in. You'll have to excuse me for a moment. I was making cookies and then I realized Olivia wouldn't be here and Mackenzie never eats my cookies. Something about carbs and fat."

Colby followed Suzanne into Mackenzie's home. This was what a home should feel like, she decided. Not a mess of collections, like her parents' house had been, or a stark place to lay your head when you had to leave work for fear people would realize you didn't really have a life, like her own condo.

"I like carbs and fat," Colby called out to Suzanne's retreating back. Mackenzie frowned at her. "Especially together. In a cookie." Mackenzie's frown deepened, and Colby looked at the floor and muttered, "Well, I do."

"When's the last time you had a cookie? I mean a real chocolate chip, mess up your clothes, too hot to eat without blowing, crumble in your mouth, cookie?" Mackenzie asked.

"Two years ago. It was mislabeled as sugar free," Colby admitted reluctantly.

"That's what I thought. What's wrong with you?"

"You didn't tell me your mom was hot!" Colby said. "She looks like Wonder Woman."

Mackenzie's mouth fell open. "Did you just call my mom hot? Like, right in front of me? In my own house?"

"Oh my God, shush. She's going to hear you."

"Well, if she didn't, I'm going to go tell her what you said." By the time Colby registered Mackenzie was about to embarrass her thoroughly, Mackenzie was already halfway across the room. A few seconds more and she would be in the kitchen telling her mom what Colby said. Mackenzie glanced back with a smile on her face and called out, "Hey, Mom, Colby thinks—"

Horrified, Colby reacted without thinking. She launched herself at Mackenzie's back, wrapped her legs around her waist, and clapped a hand over her mouth. It was a tossup as to who was more stunned, but Colby was already committed, so she whispered in Mackenzie's ear. "I am a guest in your home. You are not supposed to embarrass me!"

Mackenzie mumbled something Colby couldn't make out.

"Look, if I move my hand, do you promise not to yell?"

Mackenzie nodded, and Colby slowly began to remove her hand.

"Mom, Colby—"

Colby clamped her hand over Mackenzie's mouth and her body shook with stifled laughter. "You are a big fat liar," Colby growled.

Mackenzie began licking the palm of Colby's hand with slow, lingering swipes of her tongue in an obvious effort to gross her out. Colby narrowed her eyes and leaned close to Mackenzie's ear. "Oh yes, keep doing that. It feels so good, baby." Mackenzie froze, and it was Colby's turn to laugh.

"Okay," she said after she had calmed down. "Are you going to be reasonable about this?"

In a move that would have made a contortionist jealous, Mackenzie turned the upper part of her body, leaned over, and pulled Colby around until they were facing each other, Colby straddling Mackenzie's waist. *How much time could we have had together if we had only recognized that we had something special?*

Mackenzie's cocky smile faded, and Colby had the uncomfortable feeling that Mackenzie had read her mind. A thump behind them drew their attention from each other. Suzanne was standing in the doorway wide-eyed, a plate of cookies in her hand. Colby was afraid to look at Mackenzie. *God, we must look like two idiots.* She dropped her feet down so they weren't sticking out like a child on a swing set, but Mackenzie was too stunned to take the hint.

Mackenzie looked at her mother and grimaced. "Hey, Mom, we were just...um, playing."

"Put me down, Mackenzie," Colby whispered urgently.

"So I assume board games are probably too tame for you two, huh?" Suzanne asked and Colby wished fervently for something she could hide behind.

"Mackenzie, would you please put me down?" Finally, her

words must have sunk in. Mackenzie slid her to the floor and whispered, "Sorry."

"Cookie?" Suzanne held out the plate of warm cookies.

Without hesitation, Colby reached out and took a cookie, bit into it, and then took another bite before she had even swallowed the first. Mackenzie did the same. Good to know she wasn't the only one who reached for the sweet stuff when she got nervous. "So, how about that board game?" Colby said too brightly.

"Sure," Mackenzie said and with lecherous grin directed toward Colby, she added, "I bet Colby would love to play Twister with you, Mom."

Colby choked on her cookie.

CHAPTER TEN

Brandt Residence

"I think there's cocaine in these," Colby mumbled around a mouthful of cookie. She had gotten over her initial embarrassment at getting caught horsing around with Mackenzie and had warmed up to Suzanne. And Suzanne loved anyone who would polish off a whole plate of her cookies. If Colby had spent any time at all thinking about what Mackenzie Brandt's mother might be like, she would have missed the boat entirely. She would not have pictured a woman with such a kind smile and gentle disposition.

"If sugar and butter are cocaine, then yup, she's your pusher." Mackenzie was grinning. She had stopped eating cookies over an hour earlier.

All three of them were sprawled on the floor around Mackenzie's coffee table, drinking cocoa, eating cookies, and watching the remaining fireworks light up the sky. Thankfully, Mackenzie had been unable to find Twister. Instead, they had spent the rainy Fourth of July playing board games and watching made-for-TV movies. Mackenzie proved to be quite good at Scrabble, and Suzanne had acquired Boardwalk, Park Place, and all the orange properties in Monopoly before the closing credits of *The New Adventures of Pippi Longstocking*. When the sound of fireworks from the fair reached the house, they opened the drapes to enjoy the sable sky rent with explosions of color.

"I didn't use that much sugar," Suzanne said. "Ooh, that was a huge one!"

They were temporarily distracted by the colorful bloom that lit the sky before Mackenzie said, "You forget, I took the trash out after dinner. I saw all those empty bags."

"Bags? As in more than one? You used more than one bag of sugar?" Colby said.

"Of course I did," Suzanne said proudly. "They're sugar cookies."

Colby imagined a roll of fat forming around her middle. "I must have eaten six before dinner, and I have no idea how many I ate during the movie."

Suzanne was placing the multicolored money and game pieces in their respective places in the box. "Who are you going to believe, Mackenzie or her mother?" Mackenzie was looking at Colby over the top of Suzanne's head. Colby decided she liked the way she felt right at that moment. Comfortably sugar-stuffed and cared for. When Mackenzie's smile deepened, Colby wondered if she had given herself away. Maybe shown too much. Was there such a thing as showing too much? What difference did it make if Mackenzie knew she enjoyed spending time with her in her home?

"She's played cards with you, Mom. She knows you can't be trusted." Mackenzie put her hand on Colby's shoulder. "You're not getting bored, are you?"

Mackenzie removed her hand too quickly for it to have been casual. She had forgotten, as had Colby, that things had changed between them. Not that their touches had ever been casual, Colby thought regretfully.

"This is the most fun I've had in a long time," Colby said, and she realized it was. For the most part, she had no more friends than she had in high school. She spent her days working and her nights thinking about work. Before today, she couldn't remember the last time she'd played a board game or sat around watching

TV and stuffing her face on a rainy Friday. Colby thought that she could easily get used to this, and that scared her silly.

Suzanne groaned as she got to her feet and yawned. "I swear, the older I get, the more I feel like Olivia. I need my sleep or I get grumpy."

"I'll see you tomorrow?" Colby stood and self-consciously hugged Suzanne.

"Absolutely. I'm making pancakes, so I hope you have an appetite in the morning." Colby waited until Suzanne disappeared up the stairs.

"Um, we didn't scare her off, did we?" Colby sat on the couch instead of returning to the floor. Now that they were alone, Colby felt like she could use some space between herself and Mackenzie. "I don't see how anyone can sleep with all those fireworks going off out there."

"You can set a clock by her. Nine o'clock and she's in bed and won't be awakened by anything short of a natural disaster. I wish Olivia went down so easily." Mackenzie's smile was replaced by a distracted frown.

"What's wrong? Are you worried about Olivia?"

"Not really. I'm sure she's having a blast with her dad."

Mackenzie got up from the floor and sat on the opposite end of the couch from Colby. They enjoyed the fireworks for a few moments, commenting here and there over more spectacular ones when it seemed appropriate, and tried to act like the incongruity between them didn't exist. It made Colby sad that things had degenerated so much between them that they couldn't have fun with each other without a chaperone present. They had done things backward. They'd had sex before they got to know each other. The rules said a relationship was impossible if you had sex first. So what was she doing sitting on the woman's couch making small talk? What did she hope to gain by even being there?

"Okay, I'm going to admit something really selfish," Mackenzie said.

Colby angled her body, tucking her foot beneath her leg so that she could give Mackenzie her full attention.

"I think I'm jealous Olivia might be having more fun watching the fireworks with her dad than she has with me."

Colby chuckled in relief. Petty jealousies, she understood. She was pleased to finally find a chink in Mackenzie's nice armor, and it made her all the more attractive. Not that she needed any help in that department. "I'm no expert, but that's normal, isn't it?"

Mackenzie sighed. "I don't know, but it makes me feel like crap. I want my daughter to have fun with her dad, but to the same degree..."

"You don't want her to forget about the fun she has with you?"

"I sound very selfish when you put it like that."

"Not *very* selfish. Just...well, you know, a little selfish." Colby smiled when Mackenzie rolled her eyes. Mackenzie's jealousy was perhaps petty, but it was also cute and human.

"I wish I hadn't told you. Now I feel bad," Mackenzie grumbled.

"Oh, come on, it's not like I'm not guilty of selfish stuff."

Mackenzie kicked her shoes off and tucked her feet beneath her. "Oh, really? Do tell. I told you mine."

Colby shook her head and then she remembered something that still made her feel bad even though it had happened years ago.

"Okay, well, when I was about twelve years old, my parents—"

"No fair bringing up stuff from childhood," Mackenzie interrupted.

"Wait." Colby held up her hands. "This one is particularly bad. I mean, the devil himself is coming to pick my ass up for this one."

Mackenzie laughed quietly. "That bad, huh? Okay, but if this story isn't up to par, I reserve the right to decide whether you also tell me an adult story."

"Okay, deal. As I was saying, when I was twelve my parents split up. My dad moved into this dinky little apartment about twenty miles outside of town, and my mother, well, she pretty much cried herself to sleep every night."

"That must have been hard on you." The serious look on Mackenzie's face almost made Colby regret telling the story, but she continued.

"Actually, I loved it."

Mackenzie's brow rose, but Colby kept speaking. Now that she had started, she couldn't seem to stop. "My father picked me up from school every Friday and took me to dinner and a movie and anything else I wanted to do. Whatever extra money he had, he spent on me. Before that, we never spent time together. There was never any money to do things like go to a movie just because. My mother went from hardly ever cooking to cooking every night. Washing my clothes, doing the dishes, keeping the house clean, and showing an interest in what I did at school. Everything I thought everyone else's mother did, she was now doing. After the split, they were vying for my affection and I soaked it up. It was three months of heaven. Then one day, I came home from school and they were standing in the living room wearing huge smiles. There were wineglasses and takeout containers on the coffee table. I clearly remember thinking, I'm going to have to clean that up. Then they told me the great news. They were reconciling."

At some point during her "selfish story" Mackenzie had started to stroke her arm lightly. "And that's it; we all lived happily ever after." Colby grinned, but Mackenzie didn't smile back.

"It doesn't sound like you did."

Colby shrugged, caught off guard by how serious Mackenzie had become. "I was fine. My parents were nice people. I always had a roof over my head, and we had enough money to buy food. The other stuff wasn't necessary."

"Come here," Mackenzie said, and before Colby could protest, Mackenzie had pulled her into a hug.

Even though Colby would have liked nothing better than to be able to relax into the embrace, she couldn't. "If you start singing 'Hush Little Baby,' I'm out of here," she murmured into Mackenzie's shoulder.

"What you described was a child needing attention. We were all like that when we were kids. At that age, I doubt you understood the full ramifications of your parents breaking up. You weren't upset because they were getting back together; you were upset because the attention you'd finally been getting was about to be taken away. Your response was totally natural."

Mackenzie was rhythmically rubbing Colby's back, comforting her as if the loss had been significant and not just the tantrum of a child, as if it had happened yesterday and not years before.

"You are too good at this," Colby said.

"What?" Mackenzie sounded too soft, too caring for Colby's comfort, so she pulled away. Colby saw her reflection mirrored in Mackenzie's dark eyes, and completely forgot what she was going to say.

Colby didn't realize she was going to kiss Mackenzie until their lips were a breath apart. Mackenzie inhaled, her body tensed, and her hands went gently to Colby's forearms. Colby knew Mackenzie was trying to stop her. She knew it and she kissed her anyway. *Last time,* she thought, *make it last forever.* And then all rational thought went out the window. They jumped as a firework whistled and then exploded, but the kiss continued unbroken.

Mackenzie's mouth opened cautiously beneath hers. Colby knew at any moment, Mackenzie would put a stop to their kiss. She knew they would mutter apologies and go back to their respective ends of the couch. So when she placed a hand on

Mackenzie's chest and pressed gently, she expected Mackenzie to stop her. When she didn't, Colby pressed until Mackenzie was lying flat on the couch. Colby lay on top of her and quickly lost herself in the heat of their kiss.

Mackenzie's heart was pounding hard enough for Colby to feel it through their shirts. Her lips opened willingly beneath Colby's. Mackenzie was responding, asking for more, but Colby couldn't escape the knowledge that Mackenzie had already told her their brief affair was over. Colby stilled and lifted her head. Mackenzie's lips were parted and moist. They locked gazes. Colby felt as if her whole world had stabilized. The slow twist of arousal that had begun with the kiss continued to gather strength. Even the fireworks seemed to be on pause as Colby waited for Mackenzie to tell her to get off her.

"Open your legs for me." When Mackenzie didn't react immediately, Colby repeated herself, this time adding a "please" to the request. Mackenzie licked her lips and parted her legs and Colby fell between them. Her hips fit perfectly. All she had to do was—

Careful. The thought was enough to keep her from rushing past slow to the inevitable pleasure that, at least physically, they both wanted. She didn't touch Mackenzie's breasts the way she wanted to. Instead, Colby stroked the side of Mackenzie's neck, caressed her ear, and kissed her as if it would be their last kiss: slow, soft, wet, and loving.

The kiss went on for either an hour or a minute. Eventually, the heat they were generating became uncomfortable. Colby shifted her body to ease the tension and went rigid as Mackenzie arched up. Colby was afraid if their kiss ended, Mackenzie would have the millisecond it would take for her to remember this wasn't what she said wanted. Mackenzie lifted her hips once more, this time pressing her hand at the small of Colby's back, urging her closer. Colby pressed her forehead into Mackenzie's shoulder and tried to ignore the ringing in her ears.

Her hands were balled into fists beneath Mackenzie's

shoulders as she tried to understand what was happening. This wasn't her fault, was it?

Colby's ardor receded slightly. Mackenzie had made it clear she didn't want this kind of relationship with her, but when she felt Mackenzie's palms, calloused from weight training, ease beneath the waistband of her jeans, beneath her underwear and over her ass, all bets were off. Any doubts Colby had as to who was adding tinder to the fire between them were dashed to hell when Mackenzie squeezed her ass firmly.

Dry fucking. Her mind latched on to the crass term. Colby didn't even know why it was something that would stick in her mind. It was one of many things that girls whispered about in locker rooms. She had never been one of the ones whispering. She didn't have those kinds of friends, but she had overheard. My God, they were right. If they kept this up, she really was going to come while fully dressed.

Colby dug her fingers into the cushions of the couch, using them to move their bodies even closer. Mackenzie gasped as tongues, hips, and breath dueled for a foothold for several long, agonizingly pleasurable moments. The ringing in her ears intensified. The fireworks were muffled and bland compared to the explosion building in Colby's body, and yet she was determined to hold it off because when the passion cooled, Mackenzie would remember. Colby intentionally slowed her movements. Her last time with Mackenzie had been a fervor of passion and gluttony. She wanted to remember her this time. She lifted her head to look at Mackenzie's face. Moisture glistened on her forehead, her eyes were closed, and her lips were parted. She would come soon, and Colby wanted to savor it.

Colby's ears rang with her effort to keep control, and when she sensed Mackenzie was no longer barreling toward orgasm, she deepened her thrusts. Mackenzie's answering movements stilled suddenly, and Colby knew in her heart it was over.

"Colby, the phone is ringing. I need to answer it. I asked Nick to call me. I'm sorry."

Colby nodded, and although every nerve in her body was screaming no, she quickly got off Mackenzie. Neither looked at the other as Mackenzie stumbled to her feet and hurried off in the direction of the ringing phone. Colby stood, easing her jeans away from her crotch, and went to stand in front of the huge floor-to-ceiling window. The phone rang one more time, but she didn't hear Mackenzie move toward the kitchen.

"Hey?"

Colby looked back to see that Mackenzie was watching her with a strange look on her face.

"This might take a few minutes. She'll want to tell me about her day, but I'll meet you in your room, okay?"

Mackenzie was gone before Colby could answer. She stood blinking at the place where Mackenzie had been standing. She was getting such mixed signals from her. She wasn't about to complain about this last one, but it was confusing. Colby reached for the drapes with the intention of closing them so that Mackenzie wouldn't have to.

Smoke from the fireworks created a fog that hung just above the trees. Colby cooled her moist forehead on the glass of the window and stared out at nothing. The front of her shirt was plastered to her chest. How was she going to ever forget how perfectly they fit together, or how good Mackenzie's toned body felt beneath her, or how unbelievably strong she was?

Colby's heart panged as she realized that things had already gone too far. She wanted more from Mackenzie than just a stupid chance at payback. She should have been the one to call it quits, not Mackenzie. She was the one in danger. Her mistake was in deluding herself into believing they could be just friends.

❖

Mackenzie paused with one hand on the phone and one hand on her lips. She could smell Colby. Whether it was her lotion or the soap Colby used, Mackenzie didn't know, but she did know she would never get tired of it, and that scared her. Mackenzie took a deep breath and answered the phone.

Nick didn't bother with hello. "Where the hell were you? I called ten times. Olivia is already in bed." Mackenzie could tell by the way Nick was whispering and the cadence of his breathing that he was pacing.

"We were watching the fireworks. Is she still awake? Put her on the phone." Mackenzie sat at the small kitchen table and leaned her head back. She heard Nick tell Olivia her mom was on the phone. Mackenzie was smiling even before she heard her daughter say her customary, "Hi, Mama."

"Tell me about your day, Lil Bird." Olivia began chattering away about all the foods she had eaten and the things she'd done, seen, and heard at the fair. Mackenzie oohed and aahed where appropriate and mentally translated when her daughter's excitement made her nearly unintelligible. After several minutes, Olivia's responses slowed, then finally, Mackenzie was listening to the soft sound of her breathing.

"She's asleep," Nick whispered, and Mackenzie heard the distinct sound of a door closing.

Olivia's bedroom door was always left open. In fact, Mackenzie never closed her own bedroom door and neither did her mother. If Olivia needed them during the night, one if not both of them would hear her. Mackenzie was going to mention this to Nick but decided against it. Nick and Olivia would come up with their own rules. She would mind her own business unless Olivia's safety was in jeopardy. Besides, Olivia was growing up, and at some point she would want her privacy. Maybe Mackenzie would need some privacy too. Mackenzie pushed away the fragment before it could become a full-blown thought.

"My parents called."

The casual way in which Nick brought up his parents was usually enough to make Mackenzie look for a place to sit.

"What did they say?"

"They said they forgot they had a conflict so they didn't

go out of town. They were hoping we could meet tomorrow for lunch instead of Monday."

Mackenzie's relief that they weren't backing out of the meeting entirely was replaced with apprehension. "Fine, but they need to come here."

"Well, they know I'm not living there anymore, so they said they would prefer to meet at their house." Mackenzie pressed her fingers into the deepening furrows of her brow. The Copelands' request seemed like more game playing to Mackenzie. Unfortunately, she wasn't in on any of the rules.

"That's too bad. I asked them, not the other way around. Besides, I have a guest and I think she would feel more comfortable here."

"You aren't really thinking of bringing that woman into this? I thought we were just going to talk to them?"

"I didn't bring her into it, they did. They're the ones skulking around and hiring people to investigate me as if I had committed a crime."

"They're used to protecting their interests, Mackenzie. I'm sure they just reacted without thinking it through."

"What interest do they have in this? *We* are divorcing each other. *They* don't get an opinion."

"They might have some concerns about seeing Olivia."

"Have I ever tried to prevent them from seeing Olivia in the past? Why would they have concerns now?"

"That's what we'll tell them. Maybe they just need to hear it from us."

Nick was using the placating tone he had always used when they discussed his parents. It wasn't going to work this time. "I'll just be glad to get it over with. I hope when they see Colby, they drop the pretense and cut to the chase."

"How can you trust her? I swear when I realized she was the woman I caught peeking into your window, I almost shit."

Mackenzie's lungs deflated. "What? What are you talking about? When was she looking in my window?"

"The night that new client came on to you right in front of me, remember? What was her name?"

"Jessie. She never came back," Mackenzie said in a flat voice, remembering how Jessie had come on to her with so much enthusiasm that it had made her feel uneasy.

"I thought it was her at first, until I got up close. God, I'm sorry, Mackenzie. I knew she'd put something in her pocket, but I thought it was a cell phone. Now I wonder if it was a camera. I have no idea why she would take pictures of you at work, though."

"Why didn't you tell me this before?" Mackenzie knew she sounded shrill, but she was flashing back to that night, to the things she had been doing in her office that night, and facing the window, no less. She felt sick.

"Didn't I tell you?"

Mackenzie closed her eyes. "Damn it, Nick, you didn't. I mean, you said something about her peeping in my windows at the park, but I thought you were being rhetorical."

"Yeah, well, like I said, I didn't think anything of it until I saw her with my dad at the restaurant. I mean, it wasn't like I caught her pressed up against your bedroom window. It was at the gym and she claimed to be feeling badly. Are you still there?"

Mackenzie pushed the power button and set the phone down gently. *It wasn't like I caught her pressed up against your bedroom window.*

❖

The room that Colby had been shown to earlier in the day had the same floor-to-ceiling windows as the rest of the house. The bedding was decidedly feminine though not overly so, and someone—Suzanne perhaps—had added fresh linens and flowers since Colby had last been in the room.

Colby had been waiting for Mackenzie for almost half an

hour. She'd begun to fear Mackenzie had changed her mind, except she knew from her earlier tour of the house that Mackenzie's bedroom was upstairs and she had to walk past the guest room door to get there.

Colby pictured her in the front room, head in hands, trying to decide what to do. Colby went to the window and looked out as she had in the den. Would things ever be simple between them? Colby heard the guest room door open behind her and close quietly. She hadn't realized she was so tense until her shoulders began to ache as she relaxed them.

"Before you say anything," she said quietly without turning around, "I know you're having a hard time with this, with letting me in, and I just want to tell you that I want to try to make things better between us. It's not about paybacks or anything else. I really like being with you and getting to know you better. I'll do things the way you want as long as you let me stay in your life."

There. It was done. She had given Mackenzie an out if she needed one, but she had made it clear she wasn't just in it for fun. She wanted, needed more. Colby turned around expecting to see surprise, maybe even shock. She was unprepared for the anger mixed with intense pain written across Mackenzie's face.

"You b—"

Mackenzie's voice broke, 'but she didn't need to finish the sentence. Colby shook her head to clear the confusion. "Mackenzie? What did I do?"

"Nick told me."

Nick? Colby started walking toward Mackenzie, but Mackenzie backed away quickly. If the door had not been closed behind her, Colby was sure she would have backed out into the hall and walked away.

Colby pressed her lips together tightly. "What did he tell you?" She was certain she could refute any lies Nick Copeland might have told Mackenzie. After which she was going to throttle the man silly.

"He told me you were outside my office looking in my window. He said you were there outside my gym when we…" Mackenzie's face had gone from brick red to pale.

Oh God, why didn't I tell her I was there? "Mackenzie, I can explain."

"Explain, then. Tell me it's not true. Tell me you didn't convince me to masturbate so that you could watch."

"It wasn't like that."

Mackenzie turned, and if Colby hadn't run up behind her and put her hand on the door to stop her, she would have left the room.

"Please listen to me?" Colby said to the back of Mackenzie's head.

Mackenzie didn't say anything, but she hadn't slugged Colby, so that was a start. "I did watch you. The truth is I sent someone in to see if you would come on to her."

"Jessie," Mackenzie said bitterly. She turned around, and Colby looked down in relief. She couldn't stand to look at Mackenzie's anger anymore.

"Yes. She told me you turned her down flat and I was…" Colby shook her head and trailed off before restarting. "I was just so damn happy. I saw you sitting in that chair, and you looked so good. I wanted to be with you and I couldn't. I asked you to touch yourself because it's what I wanted to do."

Colby withstood the onslaught of Mackenzie's cool gaze for several seconds longer.

"You humiliated me."

"I wasn't trying to. I swear that wasn't what I was trying to do."

"Why should I trust you? Tell me why I should ever believe you again? How do I know you didn't take pictures and give them to Arnult and Barb?"

Mackenzie's words were as devastating as a slap to the face. "Do you really think I would take pictures of you like that and give them to those people? For what gain, Mackenzie? What would I prove by showing you by yourself?"

"You should have told me what you did."

Silence was the only answer Colby was going to get. "If I had confessed to being outside your window that night, you're telling me you wouldn't have been angry?"

"Doesn't matter. You still should have told me."

"I didn't realize it was going to go as far as it did."

"Then you should have walked away."

"That's not easy to do. I know it's hard for you to understand, but it wasn't a conscious thing. I didn't set out with the intention of not telling you."

"Colby, just let it go. It's done. I want you out of my house by morning."

"You don't mean that." Colby's fingers shook as she reached for the top button of her shirt. "I never meant to humiliate you," she said as she unbuttoned her shirt and pulled it from her jeans.

"What are you doing?"

"I'm giving you the opportunity for payback."

"Is that what you think I want?"

"It's what I thought I wanted. But you know what, Mackenzie?" Colby unbuttoned her jeans while keeping eye contact with Mackenzie. "From the very moment I saw you, payback wasn't enough. I wanted to be with you. I wanted you to show me how sorry you were by making love to me, and I was damn angry with you for making me want you so much. When I stood in front of that window while you touched yourself, believe me, humiliating you was the furthest thing from my mind. I couldn't have walked away if I wanted to." Colby dropped her shirt on the floor and reached back to unfasten her bra.

"Put your shirt back on." Mackenzie's voice was laden with anger and confusion.

"No." Colby dropped her bra on top of her shirt. Her hands shook as she pushed her pants and underwear down around

GABRIELLE GOLDSBY

her knees before kicking them off. Standing there naked made her feel more exposed than she had been in her entire life. She ignored the urge to cross her arms in front of her chest. Instead, she held Mackenzie's gaze as she backed to the bed and sat down. Mackenzie's face was frozen in a mixture of anger and shock.

"I am not going to have sex with you."

"I know," Colby said. "I'm not asking you to."

"Then why are you doing this?"

"I'm giving you the opportunity to walk away while I humiliate myself." Colby touched her chest, grazing her thumbs over her nipples despite the cold fear Mackenzie would turn around and leave anyway.

"When you were doing this," Colby whispered, "all I could think of was how much I wished I was on the other side of that window."

Colby bent her knees, ignoring any trepidation about exposing herself further to Mackenzie. When she saw the way Mackenzie followed her every move, she whispered, "Come closer."

Mackenzie shook her head, but Colby knew from experience if she stayed, she *would* come closer. Colby lowered her legs to the bed, and Mackenzie looked at the ground. She didn't leave, though, and that was important.

"Look at me," Colby ordered. Mackenzie's head jerked back as if physically forced.

Colby ran her hands along her stomach while watching Mackenzie's demeanor for any indication of what she was thinking. Mackenzie's face was astonishingly blank. The only indications she was still upset were the balled fists at her sides and the rapid rise and fall of her chest.

When Colby slowly raised her fingers to her mouth and wet two of them, Mackenzie's lips parted.

Arousal melted some of the frigid anger so prevalent on Mackenzie's face. Colby trailed her glistening fingers down her chin and neck to her chest. She circled first one nipple and then the other until both were hard-tipped peaks. Mackenzie swayed.

"It's hard, isn't it? To just stand there watching when you know how much I want you. How much I wish it was your hands on me." Colby put her fingers back in her mouth and closed her eyes to escape the heat of Mackenzie's gaze. When she opened them again she took a deep, shuddering breath. Colby trailed her hands over her stomach, brushing the very top of the triangle of hair before retreating back to her breasts. Any embarrassment she had felt initially was gone. She wanted to break Mackenzie; she wanted to make her forget her anger and come to her.

Colby angled her body to give Mackenzie a better view. There was a faint sound, a sigh perhaps, and when Colby looked up, she could have sworn Mackenzie was closer. Colby slowly ran her fingers down her labia, separating herself and rubbing the side of her clit until her fingers were coated with the evidence of her extreme arousal.

"You were so wet, Mackenzie. All I wanted to do was leap through that window and drown myself in you."

Mackenzie's throat worked rapidly. Her hands were no longer clenched; her arms hung limp at her sides.

Colby's legs fell open like butterfly wings. She toyed with her proud clit until she could no longer stand the torment. When her fingers slid home, she moaned long and soft. She waited several seconds, her toes curled into the fabric of the comforter.

Mackenzie's body had gone slack. She had given up looking angry and instead was staring hungrily at the hand nestled between Colby's legs. Colby lifted her hips, and Mackenzie gave a half shake of her head as if to tell her no, but the motion was not completed.

"You see now? Can you just walk away?" Colby saw the wild look of complete arousal on Mackenzie's face. "Look at me, Mackenzie. Watch me." Now that she was confident Mackenzie wasn't going to leave, she slid first two fingers and then a third deep within herself. Mackenzie's breathing deepened with each motion of her hips.

Colby withdrew her fingers and gasped as the evidence of

her lust spilled from her body. She coated her clit with it before sinking back into herself. "When you were inside yourself like this, I was so turned on, so…" Colby swallowed as the heat and the speed of her hand increased.

Mackenzie's face was flushed, and she was swaying slightly. Colby tilted her hips up for better access and to give Mackenzie a better view. Colby's hand was making a soft clapping sound as she gave herself no quarter.

"Can you leave me? Can you walk away while I'm doing this, while I am imagining that it's you touching me? Mackenzie, I…"

What the hell had she been about to say? She was saved from confessing feelings she didn't know she had by the onslaught of her orgasm. Colby lifted her hips and groaned, and this time she was certain Mackenzie groaned too. Liquid heat spilled from her body and the pleasure peaked, ebbed, and then seemed to peak again. Colby's moans had turned to gasping breaths, and Mackenzie's lips were parted; her chest rose and fell along with Colby's until they were gazing dumbstruck at each other.

"Mackenzie?"

Mackenzie shook her head. "Don't! You made your point." Mackenzie sounded acidic and biting. The perspiration on Colby's stomach cooled.

"I'm sorry. I just thought if I showed you how hard it was to walk away, you would understand why I couldn't."

"You know what I think? I think we spend way too much time apologizing to each other." If Mackenzie had sounded anything but tired and resigned, Colby might have known what to say. Instead, her chest ached and she was at a loss.

Mackenzie turned away. "Where are you going?" Colby blurted as she sat up, grabbing her shirt form the floor.

"I need some sleep. I'm not thinking clearly."

"I didn't mean to upset you."

Mackenzie nodded and without looking at Colby, turned and left the room, shutting the door behind her with a near-silent click. Colby stared at the closed door and shivered at the finality in Mackenzie's voice. Colby thought about packing her bags to leave, but she couldn't bring herself to do it. She was confused, scared, and ashamed. Even with all those feelings, she couldn't leave without talking to Mackenzie at least one more time. She had handled the situation poorly. It was important to her that Mackenzie believed she wasn't out to hurt her. Whether she could do that remained to be seen, but of one thing she was certain: She had lost something important tonight.

Mackenzie's trust.

CHAPTER ELEVEN

The next morning, the throb in her temples and the dull pain in her back told Mackenzie she had slept way past seven o'clock. She groaned and turned on her back. The memory of last night returned with cold vengeance.

Colby. She couldn't think about her without feeling the sting of betrayal, the heat of anger. Why hadn't she just walked out of that room last night? She had been so furious and yet it was as if she were frozen in place. Colby had made her point. It didn't make Mackenzie feel any less exposed. Anger couldn't prevent her from feeling the dull ache in her chest. Colby was gone. She had told her she wanted her out of her house. Out of her life.

Mackenzie laid the back of her wrist on her forehead. The sound of pots and pans being removed from cabinets drifted up through the heat vents. Saturday was the day her mother made her famous pancakes and homemade marionberry syrup. Mackenzie wasn't looking forward to explaining why Colby wouldn't be joining them for breakfast. It took another fifteen minutes before she stumbled into the shower. She scrubbed until her skin was pink from the rough treatment. She would never admit Colby was right, but she hadn't been able to walk away even when she was so damn angry. It still didn't excuse what Colby did. She still should have told her she had been there that night.

The water was tepid and her fingers pruned by the time Mackenzie emerged from the shower. A glance at her reflection in the partially steamed mirror dispelled any hope that her mother wouldn't guess things hadn't gone well with her and Colby. Her mother would take one look at her red-rimmed, swollen eyes and want a full explanation.

Mackenzie pulled on jeans and a T-shirt and reminded herself she would have to change before lunch with the Copelands. She dragged down the stairs, past the closed guest room door, and toward the kitchen. She wasn't looking forward to putting anything in her mouth except hot coffee. She walked into the kitchen and froze. Colby's knife paused midair. If possible, Colby looked worse than she did. Her mother would put two puffy eyes together with two puffier eyes and come up with a lovers' spat. Mackenzie wished that was all it was.

"Sit down. I warmed your plate." Her mother set the plate right next to Colby. Mackenzie didn't want to sit next to her; she didn't want to be in the same room with her. What was she still doing here, and why did her heart leap like that when she saw her?

"Oh, shoot, we're out of syrup. I'll need to get some from the pantry."

"I'll get it." Mackenzie stood, grateful for the chance to escape.

"No, stay here with Colby. She's not feeling well this morning." Her mother frowned as she left the kitchen. "Actually, you look like you might have caught a little something too."

"I'm sorry," Colby said without looking up from her plate once they were alone.

"You said that last night," Mackenzie said as she cut into her pancake. Most Saturdays Mackenzie would knock over her own daughter to get to a pancake breakfast. This morning the idea of actually swallowing one made her queasy, but if her mother hadn't already figured out something was wrong between her and Colby, she would know for sure if Mackenzie didn't clean her plate.

"I meant, I'm sorry that I'm still here."

Mackenzie set her fork carefully on her napkin and gave Colby her full attention. "You're right, I expected you to be gone by now."

"I know, and that's why I'm sorry." When Colby looked up briefly, it was all Mackenzie could do not to wince. Colby looked as if she had spent the night crying or going several rounds with a heavyweight. "I was trying to prove a point and instead I humiliated myself. I wanted you to know that I understand how you feel. I know it doesn't make things better, but…" Colby looked down at her plate, and Mackenzie finally picked up on the slumped shoulders and the fact Colby was having a hard time looking her in the face. *She is really embarrassed.* Anger aside, she hadn't meant to make Colby feel as if she had done anything wrong. Sure, it had made Mackenzie's night hell thinking about what she should have done and said. But she would be lying if she said that some part of her, a big part, had not enjoyed watching.

Since Colby wouldn't look at her, Mackenzie used the opportunity to study her body language. The way Colby was sitting left her disquieted. She looked as if she was trying to make herself appear smaller so as to go unnoticed. Mackenzie was reminded of how Colby had walked around the halls of Roheibeth High. She never realized it until now, but it had always frustrated her that she could sense a firecracker hidden beneath all that meekness.

"I think your mother knows we had a…"

Mackenzie understood Colby's hesitation. What did you call what they had? Was it an argument, or a lovers' quarrel? Were they lovers? All because Mackenzie had been embarrassed Colby had watched instead of just listened while she had an orgasm? It's not as if she would have stopped if she had known Colby was there. She'd spent most of last night imagining that very thing. Mackenzie's face flushed.

She put her hand on Colby's arm. "Look at me, please."

When Colby looked at her, Mackenzie noted the sadness and the confusion, and her heart melted. "I think I might have overreacted."

Colby's smile was self-deprecating. "I'm the one guilty of overreacting."

Mackenzie swallowed. "Colby, you and I have been on the wrong foot since the reunion. Actually, that's the problem. We haven't spent much time on our feet. When I found out you were watching me I was really embarrassed. No, wait, let me finish." Mackenzie put her hand up to stop Colby before she could speak. "You've apologized enough. That's not why I'm saying all this." She took a deep breath. "You and I are not friends." Colby slumped in her chair. Several seconds passed before Mackenzie went on. "And we should be. I think we could have been friends in high school, but I was dealing with so much at home that I guess I just lashed out at everyone."

"Why didn't you just come up to me and say hello?"

"You mean you don't know?" Colby shook her head and Mackenzie smiled sadly. "I had a thing for you."

Colby's mouth dropped. "Lara said that at the reunion. I thought she was drunk."

"She said that? I wish she would have told me. Back then I didn't understand why I had it out for you. I just knew you bugged the shit out of me. My father must have picked up on a gay vibe or something because he figured it out long before I did."

"Really? I didn't see any evidence of it."

"Could have been all the female sports figures I had plastered all over my bedroom walls. I don't know. One moment we were best friends, and the next I was like a red flag and he was a bull. He charged at the mere sight of me. He'd call me queer, and right before I moved out he started telling me I was going to hell for having the feelings I was having. I hadn't told anyone, but it felt like everyone knew anyway. Things got worse after I was expelled."

Colby looked stricken. "I always felt guilty about that. I should have said something that day."

Mackenzie shrugged. "It wouldn't have done any good. I made it easy to find a reason to expel me. I was just so confused. I didn't understand what it was about me that he hated so much. I was acting out because I was confused."

"What about your mother?"

"Well, as you might imagine, she was too busy trying to keep her marriage together to realize what I was going through. My father was not an easy man to live with. I loved him, but he was just as hard on my mother as he was on me. I don't think she realized how much the things he said hurt me. She's changed a lot since the divorce. She and I never had the opportunity to become close. I think she sees helping me with Olivia as a way to make things right."

"Is that why you married Nick? To please your father?"

Mackenzie sighed. "I did a lot of things to please my father. I wanted him to be proud of me. It was the sole reason I joined the military. So yeah, I guess I may have married Nick to please my father. Nick and I were already roommates and he's my best friend. I told myself I was doing him a favor. He wanted to get his parents off his back, and I wanted...I wanted to make my father happy. It was probably one of the stupidest things either of us will ever do. We were each looking for a way to fit in with our own family and we found that way in each other. I think that back in high school I saw it in you, but I didn't know how to reach out to you. With Nick it was easy—there was no attraction."

"I wish we could have talked like this when we were younger."

"You mean you didn't enjoy leaping past the talk stage and going straight to watching each other masturbate?"

Colby's back straightened and she looked toward the door.

"What's the matter? You don't want my mother to know you *masturbate*? It's a good thing she didn't see us making out on the couch last night."

"Would you be quiet? She'll be back any minute now." Colby sounded exasperated, but her expression gave away her relief.

"She won't be back anytime soon. She knows we've been fighting. She's giving us the chance to talk."

"I didn't tell her anything."

Mackenzie raised a brow. "You didn't have to. Mothers know these things." She got another smile out of Colby, and her heart did a shameless little leap.

"Mackenzie, what did you mean earlier when you said we weren't friends?"

"I meant we don't really know each other. I don't know what I am to you. I mean, my in-laws hired you to find dirt on me and you took the job." Mackenzie held up her hands. "I know you told me you gave the check back and I believe you, I do, but I can't forget that you first agreed to do the job. And it still doesn't negate the fact that you and I have done nothing but be mad at or have sex with each other—ever. There doesn't seem to be an in-between for us. I have a feeling, and a hope, there's more to us than that, which is why I can't continue to just sleep with you."

"What does that *mean*?" Mackenzie heard Colby's disappointment and forced her own tone to stay light.

"I'm not completely sure."

"Then what makes you think there's more to us?"

"Because I feel it."

❖

If Mackenzie noticed Colby was quiet throughout the morning, she pretended otherwise, as did Suzanne. There had been no more talk of Colby leaving. She had even helped with some of the lunch preparation and had listened quietly while Suzanne and Mackenzie discussed everything from the gym to Olivia.

Colby had never thought she would be good with kids, but

for some reason that little girl had taken a liking to her. The moment she walked into the house she had run to Colby, her arms wide. Colby had been unprepared for the smack of Olivia's little head in her abdomen, but she thought she recovered well, even managing to pat the little girl on the back. She looked to Mackenzie for help, but Mackenzie was too busy taking Olivia's things from Nick and asking him how things had gone.

Colby gently extricated herself from Olivia's arms and squatted because she thought that was what she was supposed to do with kids. "Hi, did you have fun?" Olivia nodded and launched into a dizzying account of her evening with her dad that left Colby trying to catch her breath. Suzanne eventually came from the kitchen and whisked the little girl away for a story and a nap.

When Colby noticed that both Nick and Mackenzie were watching her, she said hesitantly, "She's a great little girl." She was amazed by the twin looks of pride that flashed across their faces. Colby still had issues with Nick. She didn't like the way he seemed to be letting Mackenzie take the brunt of everything, but she had no doubts he loved his daughter and would be there for her.

"I called my parents on the way over. They were finishing up the last two holes at the club. They should be here in an hour or so." Nick looked at Mackenzie's jeans, T-shirt, and Keen slip-ons. "You are going to change, aren't you?"

Colby almost said something in Mackenzie's defense but didn't. She had no right to insert herself into this discussion.

"Actually," Mackenzie said, "I *had* planned on changing, but I won't be putting on an outfit like the one you have on. Who dressed you, your mother?"

Colby grinned at Nick's pastel pink golf shirt, white pants, and matching white deck shoes. He did indeed look like he had been dressed by Barb Copeland.

"I'll have you know your daughter helped me pick this out."

Mackenzie narrowed her eyes. "Liar. Olivia hates pink, and if your pants were any tighter you'd have to put a rated R over your crotch. That's a Barb special and you know it."

Nick looked down at his clothing, and to Colby's surprise, he laughed. "They're not that bad, but you'd think after all these years she'd know my size. Isn't it a freaking horrendous outfit, though? I think she bought everything the model was wearing in the catalog photo. I got it in the mail last Christmas, remember? Store wrapped, with a card written in someone else's handwriting."

"Yeah, I just had no idea how bad it was. Hey, didn't a matching neckerchief come with it?"

"Don't push it," Nick said with affection, and Colby realized Mackenzie and Nick had found a comfortable path in their relationship. They interacted with each other as brother and sister rather than husband and wife. Colby still didn't quite get what Mackenzie had gained from the marriage. They could have had Olivia together anyway. But she did understand a desire for family and belonging. She had pushed that desire to the back of her mind as she had grown older, but it was still there.

❖

Colby was finding it hard not to overanalyze what Mackenzie said about them "having more" as she slowly dressed for the meeting with the Copelands. The truth of the matter was she did feel something for Mackenzie. If she didn't, she would have taken the out Mackenzie had given her and gone back to Portland. It would have been easier emotionally. She wouldn't have had to confront her own feelings if she had, but she couldn't leave things unfinished.

Colby gave herself the once-over in the mirror. She knew she looked professional, maybe even attractive, but putting on the work attire had made her feel out of sorts. Mackenzie had not requested that she change, but she knew without being told that the Copelands would look down on anyone wearing jeans.

Colby stayed in the guest room as long as she could before returning to the den, where Mackenzie hoped a civilized conversation would take place.

Mackenzie had said she would change clothes, but Colby had no idea she meant she would change so completely. Gone was the girl in the baggy jeans and sweatshirts. Gone was the attractive fitness professional. Mackenzie had made a chameleon-like U-turn and Colby didn't know where to rest her gaze. Mackenzie had always been beautiful. Even in high school when she did her best to look sullen and unapproachable, Colby would have been hard-pressed not to find her attractive. Mackenzie's hair was pinned back behind a fashionable piece of leather. She was wearing light linen pants, backless sandals, and a tank top. Colby lingered on Mackenzie's powerful shoulders and arms. She wished she had a right to walk over and kiss her, tell her that everything was okay, but she didn't. In fact, what right did she have to even be there? This was family business, and she wasn't part of the family. *No, but I'd like to be.*

Almost as if she had heard the thought, Mackenzie looked up and caught her staring. They were saved from an uncomfortable moment by the door chime.

"I'll get it," Nick said and took off as if Mackenzie or Colby were going to beat him to the door.

Colby walked over to Mackenzie and put a hand on the back of hers. "Don't worry, okay?"

Mackenzie looked away from the door long enough to smile wanly at Colby. "I'm glad you didn't leave last night."

Colby was saved from overanalyzing Mackenzie's statement by two querulous-sounding voices and one placating one.

Arnult and Barb stepped into the room as if they paid the mortgage. It was obvious from their matching striped Penguin shirts and white pants that the Copelands had interrupted their golf game to attend lunch with their son and soon-to-be ex daughter-in-law.

The awkward moment Colby was expecting when the couple realized who she was never came.

"Ms. Dennis, how have you been?" Arnult said as casually as he would have if they had run into each other in the frozen food section of the supermarket.

Colby got over her shock enough to dip her chin in what she hoped would pass as a nod. Nick's face had gone pale, and she didn't dare look at Mackenzie. The Copelands were not surprised to see her there. *Which means they knew I was here. The only way they could know that is if someone is reporting back to them already.* Colby's stomach roiled at the idea of being the one spied upon. She wanted to ask the Copelands who the hell they thought they were, but she stifled the urge. This wasn't about her. She was there to support Mackenzie if needed. Otherwise, she was determined to keep her mouth shut.

"I suppose we aren't here for lunch, are we? That's too bad. I am feeling a bit peckish." Barb Copeland managed to sound put-upon and amused at the same time. Colby was gradually forming a very different opinion of her, and it wasn't an improvement.

"Want me to make you a drink, Mom?" Nick asked.

"I said I was hungry," Barb said sharply as she looked at her watch. "Not thirsty. Besides, it's not quite two yet."

Nick looked so confused Colby had to stifle a laugh. His face said clearly what he could not say aloud: *Since when have you let the hour dictate when you had a drink?*

"My mother and I did prepare lunch, but we hoped we could talk first." Mackenzie sounded so calm Colby took the opportunity to look at her. Unlike Nick's, Mackenzie's face was calm. Actually, carefully blank would be a more appropriate description. "Won't you two sit down?"

Colby noticed for the first time that someone had brought more chairs into the room. She took the one closest to Mackenzie.

"You obviously haven't asked us here just for a meal, so what is this about?" Arnult asked.

Again, it was Mackenzie who spoke. "It's about you hiring people to investigate me." Arnult's brow shot up in mock surprise, and Colby was sure her own brow did the same. She didn't exactly expect small talk, but she hadn't expected Mackenzie to get right to the point.

"Frankly, I'm amazed Ms. Dennis would think so little about her client's confidentiality."

"Actually, Colby didn't tell us. I saw you at the hotel, remember?" Colby swiveled her head to look at Nick, who was sitting on the other side of Mackenzie. *Interesting that Nick would speak up for me.*

"Did she also tell you she was sleeping with your wife?" Barb Copeland asked conversationally.

"No, she didn't," Nick said. "Mackenzie let that one out of the bag."

Colby gave a mental cheer for Nick. She didn't necessarily like the guy, but he was trying, and he got a brownie point if only for the shocked look that flashed across Barb's face. Colby realized her family dynamic was as complicated as a crossword on the back of a cereal box compared to these people.

"Still, I don't think it at all appropriate that she be here." Finally Arnult directed his comments directly to Colby. "Do you always take such a hands-on approach with your clients?"

Colby wondered at the shift of attention to her, realized Arnult was trying to get his bearings, and decided not to give it to him. "Yes, I do. Every last one." She smiled at the shocked look on his face. *End of conversation, asshole. This isn't about me and you know it.*

"What was it you hoped to gain by having me investigated?" Mackenzie finally asked. "Nick and I have already told you our relationship is over."

"You were divorcing our son," Barb said.

"It's an amicable divorce."

"Divorces are never completely amicable. We want to make sure Nick is protected even if he is too ignorant to protect his own interests."

"Thank you, Mother," Nick said bitterly. Colby could tell by the darkening of his skin that being called dumb in front of people probably wasn't a new occurrence.

"It's what parents do," Barb said graciously.

"That's what I don't understand. How is it that you believe I'm a danger to Nick? His name is no longer on the title of the house. He has visitation with Olivia anytime he wants, and all of his child support goes to her college fund. What is it you think I'm going to take away from him?"

Colby's reaction was instinctive. She reached and Mackenzie's hand was there. Colby looked at her briefly. The frustration on her face made Colby ache to pull her into a hug.

Barb opened the large bag she had been carrying and pulled out a file folder. "When you become a parent," she said conversationally, "you lose your opportunity to have fun."

"Are *you* lecturing *me* on how to be a parent?" Mackenzie's face was no longer carefully blank. She was quite obviously livid. Venom dripped from every word that wrestled itself from her tight lips.

"Mother, you shouldn't," Nick said weakly.

"You're damn right she shouldn't. Let me tell you something. My daughter will never be afraid to come to me. She won't dread having to have dinner with me once a month, and she won't have to consider my feelings with every decision she makes as an adult." Colby was ready to stand up and cheer Mackenzie, but Barb seemed thoroughly unimpressed. Colby couldn't tell if Barb Copeland had even heard a word Mackenzie had said.

"How do you think she'll feel when she sees this?" Barb opened the file and laid it on the coffee table. They all leaned over and looked at the picture of Mackenzie walking across the street laughing at something her companion had said. Colby stifled a pang of jealousy. It was obvious that the two were coming from a nightclub. Both were smiling, and Colby couldn't help but think they looked good together.

Barb moved the picture aside and showed another with an unfamiliar car parked in front of Mackenzie's house and the same car parked there in the morning. Colby's face heated. "When we realized the nature of what we were dealing with, we thought we had better find someone with a little more discretion." Barb sat back and glanced at Colby. "Or tried to, anyway."

So I wasn't the first person the Copelands hired to spy on Mackenzie.

Colby looked at Mackenzie expecting to see the anger, not a look of utter disgust. Mackenzie shook her head. "Is that what this is all about? I don't believe this."

"Palmer is a friend of Mackenzie's," Nick said.

"Nick, you don't need to explain for me." Mackenzie turned to the Copelands and managed to sound civil. "What I do in my personal time is none of your business. Even less so now."

"You're raising our granddaughter. We don't want her embarrassed by the fact that her mother was seen coming out of a known homosexual establishment. With a—"

"Lesbian?" Colby supplied helpfully.

"Palmer stayed with us that night. She had been drinking. She stayed in the guest room. I don't know why I'm even bothering to explain anything to you."

"How convenient that you have a guest room. Is that where Ms. Dennis is staying now?" Barb made no effort to hide the fact she thought Mackenzie was using her guest room as a place to stash her girlfriends. "This, by the way, was taken *before* you filed for divorce from my son."

"Mother, I knew about this. I knew about Mackenzie going to the club, and I knew Palmer stayed here. This is Mackenzie's home. She can have anyone here she wants."

Colby was having a hard time holding her tongue. Nick was stepping in where he could, but he wasn't doing anything to take the focus off Mackenzie. He was keeping his feet clean while appearing to be valiantly helping Mackenzie.

"We don't want our granddaughter raised in this kind of environment."

Mackenzie turned around then, fear and nervousness made Colby rigid. "Your granddaughter? Tell me something, Barb. When is her birthday?" When she didn't answer, Mackenzie went on glaring at Barb Copeland as if she couldn't stand the sight of her. Colby knew that look and was glad not to be on the receiving end of it. "What's Olivia's favorite color? How about her favorite cartoon? Up to this point, you know nothing about your *granddaughter*, why in the heck are you so worried about her environment now?"

"Mother, I love my daughter. I wouldn't leave her anywhere where she wasn't safe, and Mackenzie feels the same. We appreciate your being so concerned, but this needs to stop. Now."

Look who found a backbone, Colby thought as she continued going through the file as if she were thumbing through vacation photos. Barb had several more photos of Mackenzie and her friend Palmer walking out of the club and a photo of Mackenzie waving good-bye to Palmer the next morning that was hard for Colby to look at. Then there was a picture from the night before of Colby standing in the window looking forlorn.

"What the hell?" Colby leaned forward and picked up the folder to look at the photo up close. "That's from last night? How did you…?"

Barb Copeland's mouth twisted. "Digital cameras are wonderful, I'm told."

"What is it that you really want?" Mackenzie's voice sounded tired and beat up, and Colby hated hearing it. Nick took the folder from Colby and sat back in his chair to go through it.

"We want you both to reconsider the divorce."

Both Mackenzie's and Nick's mouths dropped open, but

Mackenzie recovered faster. "Why in the hell would we do that?"

"Please watch your mouth, Mackenzie. Because we think both of you have lost sight of the big picture. Do you think we really care about your dalliances? We don't. But we"—Barb and Arnult looked at each other—"know how one bad decision can haunt you for the rest of your life. Do you have any idea how hard it will be on that little girl when you try to get her into a private school? They look at everything these days."

"In Roheibeth?" Colby blurted. She didn't even know Roheibeth had private schools, let alone ones that considered things such as marital status and sexuality when considering enrollment.

Barb went on as if she hadn't heard Colby at all. "If she doesn't get into a good preschool it will be hard to get her into the best kindergarten, and you can forget college prep."

"Are you fucking kidding me?" Mackenzie voiced Colby's thoughts perfectly.

Colby waited for Barb's reprimand, but the look on the woman's face said she had already decided Mackenzie was a lost cause. Colby liked seeing this side of Mackenzie. She had wondered when she was going to surface and now that she was there, Colby found her awe-inspiring.

"Your parents are divorced so you won't understand the importance of it, but there has never been a divorce on either side of our families. Ever. We tried to discourage Nick from marrying you so quickly, but he did. You have a child. You can't just walk away as if you never took vows."

"Vows? This isn't about vows. This isn't even about Olivia," Mackenzie said. "This is all about you and what *your* friends will think. You care more about what strangers think than you do your own son's happiness."

Arnult apparently decided Mackenzie didn't merit an answer because he directed his next question to his son. "Nick, what about your political aspirations? The people of Roheibeth aren't going to want an elected official who can't hold together his own family."

Now we get to the heart of the matter. The people of Roheibeth? Are they living in the Dark Ages? What the heck do the people of Roheibeth care if Nick is divorced? Colby thought.

Nick's fingers were laced and hanging between his legs. When he looked up, Colby saw the weariness caused by years of being told what you were going to do with your life. Her childhood, in comparison, seemed like a dream.

"Is that what this is about? I've told you, I'm not sure I want to run for office. I have enough on my plate as it is."

Colby bit the inside of her cheek. *You don't "tell them" by saying you're "not sure," rich boy.*

Arnult smiled. "You have capable employees that you trust. Let them run the day-to-day. You will need to oversee things, but at this point in your business you should be able to diversify your career."

"Did you not hear what he said? He doesn't want to run for office," Mackenzie said wearily.

Barb waved a hand in the air. "Copelands have always served in Roheibeth in some fashion or another. It's his duty. It's not about what he wants. If you insist on a divorce, no one will exactly hold it against you." Barb twisted her mouth and glanced at Colby as if she were an accident on a new carpet.

These people were serious. They had no trouble tearing their son's life apart, which meant that his wife, regardless of the fact that they were about to get a divorce, was also fair game. Mackenzie had confessed to making some mistakes in her life. Marrying Nick Copeland had to rate right up there with one of the biggest.

Nick opened the file folder again. "Did you look at all these pictures?"

Barb shuddered. "Of course not. Why would we?"

"You should. I find them all very interesting." Nick pulled

one photo and slid it across the table. "Particularly this one." Colby leaned forward, as did Mackenzie and the Copelands, to get a better look. It was a very good photo of Nick and the guy Colby had seen him with at the hotel restaurant. They were horsing around in a pool. Nick slid another one onto the table. "This one's even better." He was holding his friend close. Colby spent a moment being amazed by the details of the photo. Everything was crystal clear, right down to the water droplets poised on the tips of Nick's lashes.

"You're right," Mackenzie said softly. "He does look like Brad Pitt."

"If you continue with this, I will make sure the people of Roheibeth know exactly why Mackenzie and I get along so well." *Wow, Nick, ol' boy, you said that without moving your lips. That's really cool.*

"Nick, this is disgusting."

"Dad, what you're calling disgusting is who I am. It might be disgusting to you, but it's my life. I will not have you around my daughter if you can't respect me or her mother. I'm tired of pretending and asking my friends to pretend for me. It's over. You are going to leave Mackenzie alone or I'm outing myself on the front page of the *Roheibeth Reporter*."

If Barb could have leaned farther away from the photos she would have. As it was, Colby was afraid someone would have to breathe into her lungs to force air between her ashen lips.

Colby cleared her throat. It was time to make her contribution to the conversation. "It's well after two o'clock. I imagine you're ready for that drink now."

Chapter Twelve

"Think they'll leave us alone?" Mackenzie asked when she came back into the room after showing Barb and Arnult to the door.

Nick was lost in his own thoughts, so it was Colby who answered. "I don't know, but you nailed it with those two. They're all about appearances. As long as they think their son will come out of the closet if they make a stink, they'll stay out of your way."

Colby's attention was momentarily on Nick, and Mackenzie was grateful. Being around Colby was becoming hard. "That was really the best and only thing you could have done to nip this thing in the bud." Nick gave two hard nods of his head, but he looked as if someone had just slapped the hell out of him.

"I can't believe they know." Nick looked at Mackenzie for help.

"You knew you'd have to tell them eventually," Mackenzie said gently.

Nick blinked. "I know. I just thought I'd feel more relief." Nick slapped the top of his thighs and then rubbed them. He smiled but bemusement, not humor, was clearly written across his face. "I think this calls for a celebratory ice cream and movie. You two game?"

Colby cleared her throat. "Thanks for the offer, but I should probably get back to Portland."

Nick looked at Mackenzie, but she refused to return his gaze. Colby was looking everywhere but at her. *So this is how it ends.*

Nick stood, obviously uncomfortable with the tension in the room. "I'm going to head up and see if Suzanne and Olivia might be up for an outing. Colby, under different circumstances..." Nick stuck out his hand and Colby shook it.

Mackenzie waited until Nick left the room. "Are you sure you don't want to stay another day or so? You're more than welcome."

Colby did look at her then. Mackenzie was disappointed by what she saw.

"I prefer not to drive at night if I can help it. I better get my things." Mackenzie let Colby walk away because she didn't know what else to do. As much as she didn't want her to go, she hadn't lied to Colby. She needed more than casual sex.

Mackenzie pasted a smile on her face for her daughter's benefit, but she had a feeling Nick and her mother weren't so easily fooled. Her mother's hug lasted a little too long for her simply to be going for ice cream and a movie. Mackenzie's smile disappeared as soon as the door closed behind them. She gave Colby her space for as long as she could before it became too much and she approached the guest room. Anxiety had already twisted her insides into a mass of nerves. Mackenzie knocked, but didn't wait for Colby to say she could come in.

Colby was standing in the middle of the room with a question in her eyes. Mackenzie went to her and pulled her into her arms. The hug gave her much-needed contact, but it also stopped her from having to see Colby's confusion.

"You're making this hard," Colby said into Mackenzie's shoulder.

"I don't want it to be easy."

"But you said—"

"I *know* what I said." Mackenzie struggled with her need to make Colby understand she wasn't rejecting her. She was trying to tell her she wanted their relationship to be more than sex and arguments about who did what to whom ten years ago. She was so tired of hiding her feelings. She had been given a second chance to let Colby see who she really was, and she had failed. Mackenzie slumped and Colby's arms tightened around her as if sensing she needed her strength. Mackenzie dug her hands in Colby's hair and brought their lips together. Mackenzie poured everything she had into their good-bye kiss.

Mackenzie's throat constricted as she remembered that Colby lived three hours away, had her own business, had made no promises to her, and had made no suggestion she was even looking for more than sex from their relationship.

Sex was something Mackenzie could no longer give, but she could make love to her, perhaps show her what she couldn't say. Mackenzie tugged Colby's shirt from her pants, but when she reached for the fastener, Colby stopped her.

"Mackenzie, look at me." When Mackenzie did, she wished that she hadn't. "You're confusing the hell out of me."

"I'm confusing myself. But I want to make love to you. Right now. Please?"

Colby's arousal overcame her confusion.

Good, I don't want to talk. But we need to talk. Mackenzie pushed the last thought away as she undressed Colby fully. She took no time with her own clothes, stripping them roughly and dropping them to the floor. Every hair on her body stood up as she gently eased Colby down on the bed and lay next to her.

Mackenzie pulled Colby into another hug. She realized she was telling Colby good-bye, and it hurt more than it should have if all they had was a relationship based on casual sex. *I should tell her now. Maybe if I tell her she won't go just yet. But if I tell her and she leaves anyway…*

Colby had her payback and she didn't even realize it.

Mackenzie pushed the thought away and took Colby's areola in her mouth, working the nipple with her tongue with slow adoration until it had formed a bullet point of pleasure. Colby buried her fingers in Mackenzie's hair, urging her to continue.

Unable to wait any longer, Mackenzie wedged her body between Colby's legs and pressed her stomach briefly into the silken dampness, eliciting a moan from Colby before slipping farther down the bed. Mackenzie wrapped her arms beneath Colby's thighs, lifting her slightly so that she lay open and beautiful. Mackenzie trembled as she ran her tongue around the sensitive outer walls of Colby's labia, spreading heat and moisture before capturing Colby's clit between her lips and rapidly manipulating it with the tip of her tongue. She breathed Colby's scent in and tried to ignore her own pulsating clitoris. Deciding she had tormented both of them enough, Mackenzie cupped Colby's ass cheeks, urging her open. This time when she stroked Colby, she allowed her tongue to slip lower into the place where she could comfortably spend hours. She pushed her tongue as deep as she could go, widening it so that it brushed the walls of Colby's quivering vagina. Mackenzie took everything Colby had to offer. Colby's hips moved in a sensuous figure eight that allowed them a comfortable rhythm for several minutes.

Mackenzie almost regretted it when the caressing fingers in her hair became more insistent. Colby's hip movements were no longer controlled and her breathing had taken on a more labored quality. Mackenzie could have slowed things, giving them a few more lovely minutes together, but her own need was rising along with Colby's.

She understood completely when Colby's grip became hard and demanding. She even understood Colby's reticence for it to end when she moaned, "Oh no."

There would be no holding back now. Colby had slipped past the point of holding off and was on the verge of orgasm. Mackenzie quickly moved her hands from beneath Colby's body where she had been holding her up as if in sacrifice and eased two fingers into Colby while her tongue lifted and then soothed Colby to the brink of orgasm and then pushed her gently over the edge. When it hit, Colby arched hard. Mackenzie was ready for it and held on with one arm, her mouth refusing to leave home until she had taken every bit of Colby's pleasure as her own.

She was able to mentally block off the fire raging in her own body until cries had degenerated into soft breathing. Mackenzie lay with her head on Colby's hip, wondering how often she would be forced to relive the sound of Colby's cries of pleasure in her dreams after Colby returned to Portland. She dug her fingers into the bedclothes and eased her legs apart in an effort to avoid friction. Her breath caught as she realized her body was determined to take her to where she wasn't ready to go yet.

"Don't you dare," she heard Colby mutter, and in a shocking show of strength, Colby somehow flipped them over and inserted her thigh between Mackenzie's legs. Mackenzie tried to help, but she felt her eyelids close. She had no choice but to welcome the pleasure even though she realized that it meant the end. She either remembered or echoed Colby's "oh no" as her body leapt off the bed. Just as she did, Colby entered her with swift, sure strokes braced by her thigh. Mackenzie cried out at the welcome invasion; her body closed around Colby's fingers, refusing to let go as the orgasm started around Colby's fingers and ripped up her torso and to the top of her head before it went roaring back down through her body and ended at her curled toes.

❖

They showered, touching each other with reverence, and then they dressed without a word. Mackenzie left in silence while Colby put her remaining clothing into her bag. Finally, there was nothing else for Colby to do but leave.

Something thick and intrusive was creeping up Colby's throat as she entered the den. Mackenzie was standing in the center of the room with her arms folded. "You sure you don't want to stay for dinner? Olivia will be disappointed she didn't get to say good-bye."

Colby searched Mackenzie's face. She couldn't imagine Olivia being upset about her being gone. She had only met the child twice. Olivia had seemed very happy to see her, though. "Maybe you can tell her good-bye for me?" she asked hopefully. What did all this mean? Was she supposed to just walk out the door never to return? Mackenzie said she couldn't have that kind of relationship with her, but did that mean it was all over? "Um, can you thank Suzanne for me as well?"

Mackenzie nodded. "I will."

"Well, I'm going to get going. I probably have a ton of work waiting for me." That was a lie. Asia would have called if anything pressing had come up. There would be no demanding work to keep this ache at bay when she returned to Portland, only an apartment with empty white walls and furniture that had barely been used in a condo she had paid someone else to decorate.

"Call me when you get home?" Mackenzie looked worried, but Colby instantly felt her heart lighten. This wasn't good-bye, or at least if it was, it wasn't a complete cut-and-dry thing.

"I will. I promise."

Mackenzie reached out and put her hand on Colby's bag. Colby realized she had been holding it against her chest. Mackenzie gently took the bag from her and pulled her into the curve of her body.

She said she wants me to call her when I get back to Portland. It's not over.

Of course it's over. You live almost three hours away. She made it clear she needed more than you have to offer.

Why does this hurt so much?

Colby brushed her lips along Mackenzie's jaw-line. Both women paused, cheek to cheek, and if not for the faint ticking of a clock, Colby might have believed someone had answered her prayer that time stop. *Walk away, Colby. Just walk away.*

"I'll call you," Colby said. She felt Mackenzie's nod. She *would* call. She wouldn't be able to *not* call, but she feared that over time they would become more distant. Both of them would lose themselves in their respective businesses, and the conversations would become more and more distant before one of them, probably Mackenzie, would forget to call. Or worse, would find what she was looking for with someone else. Then there would be nothing except for the hole where her heart used to be.

Mackenzie initiated the kiss, and Colby leaned heavily into her, but Mackenzie wouldn't let her deepen the kiss. Instead, she held Colby's neck in the palm of her hand, her thumb doing that soothing thing that made Colby want to whimper. Mackenzie sipped from Colby's lips, small gentle kisses that were both sweet and incredibly painful. Colby imagined a hard tile wall pressing into her back, and the turmoil of being asked—no, *begged*, for something she didn't know how to give.

When Mackenzie finally lifted her head, Colby was reluctant to open her eyes for fear of what she would see on Mackenzie's face.

"I have something for you." Mackenzie turned away and reached for something on the couch that Colby had not noticed. Mackenzie handed over a rectangular package wrapped tightly in a paper bag and tied with white string. Her hands trembled when she handed it to Colby. She looked distant, unreadable. Colby started to open the package, but Mackenzie stopped her. "Open it when you get home. Okay?"

Colby nodded. Eyes blurring, she picked up her bag and walked out of Mackenzie Brandt's home trying to figure out why the hell she felt so damn numb.

Colby threw her bag in the backseat and placed Mackenzie's package in the front. It looked like a wrapped picture frame, but Colby didn't think it was Mackenzie's style to have given her a framed photograph.

Colby started her car and pulled onto the road. In minutes she was on the freeway to Portland, her music turned up high in order to keep her mind from finding footing where she didn't want it to. Colby turned to a nineties music station that brought back memories of high school that no longer seemed so heartbreaking. She would call Mackenzie as soon as she got home and thank her for the gift.

Colby glanced at the package in her passenger seat and wondered what it was. Mackenzie obviously wanted some kind of relationship with her or she wouldn't have given her a gift and insisted that Colby call her when she got home.

Colby drove for another five minutes, her eyes drawn to Mackenzie's gift. A sign at the side of the road told her there wouldn't be another exit for three miles after the one at Sisters Road. Colby took the exit.

Emergency brake on and car still running, Colby tore away the brown bag until she was holding a book in her hand. Colby recognized it through her tears. Mackenzie had given her a copy of their high school yearbook. She had always regretted having left hers on the bench that day. Colby opened the book, and a sob wrenched from her throat as she recognized her clumsy attempts at calligraphy on the inside flap. This wasn't a copy. This was *her* high school yearbook. The one she hadn't seen since that day in the locker room when she had caught Mackenzie scribbling inside. Colby turned to the back page and scanned the notes from kids she either barely remembered or didn't remember at all and finally found the one signed by Mackenzie.

> *In the years to come, I hope you forget my face and the sound of my voice saying things that were cruel and untrue. If you must remember anything about me, please let it be that I will always regret never having found the courage to tell you that I'm in love with you.*
> —*Mackenzie Brandt*

Colby closed the book and held it tightly against her heart. The first tear slipped past the corner of her eye at the thought of Mackenzie having these feelings for her. She'd had her crushes in school. At first on boys—it wasn't until college that she realized that girls made her heart do things that boys never did. On one level, she had recognized Mackenzie as attractive, but had she thought of her as anything but an enemy? She didn't know. Part of her was glad she hadn't found the book. She was probably too young to understand how much courage it had taken Mackenzie to write it. Especially now that she knew what she had gone through with her father.

With trembling fingers, Colby picked up her cell phone and scrolled through the incoming numbers until she found Mackenzie's. The phone rang until it went to voicemail. "Mackenzie, would you…could you call me when you get this message?" Colby left her number just in case and ended the call. Maybe she should have said more, that she had read the inscription in the yearbook, but she couldn't bring herself to put that on a voicemail. It seemed too precious a thing to risk Suzanne hearing first.

Colby opened the book again, reread Mackenzie's words, and traced the crude little heart with the arrow going through it as she tried to imagine how she would have reacted if she had read this at seventeen. Would she have been mature enough to understand?

Colby jumped when her cell phone rang, but slumped when she didn't recognize the number on her caller ID as Mackenzie's.

"Colby? I forgot to put the cordless on its base last night. The battery's dead. I'm on my cell. What's wrong?" Alarm colored Mackenzie's voice, and Colby wanted to put her at ease, but when she tried to speak only a strangled sob came out. Mackenzie said something, but it sounded as if her hand was over the mouthpiece. Colby thought she heard Suzanne answer.

"Colby, you need to calm down for me. Have you been in an accident? Are you hurt? Can you tell me where you are?"

Colby heard a car door slam and the sound of music blaring for an instant and then an expletive. "Colby, please tell me where you are?"

"I'm just off Highway Five. Sisters Road," Colby managed to get out before another sob took control.

"Okay, all right." Mackenzie sounded relieved. "Were you in an accident? Are you hurt? Did you call 911?"

Colby took a deep breath and placed her hand over her mouth until she was sure she was done crying. She didn't know what was wrong with her. Was it possible to be both happy and sad at the same time?

"I saw what you wrote in my yearbook," Colby finally choked out.

Mackenzie let out a breath. "And it made you cry like that?"

"Yes."

"Can you tell me why?"

"Because I think I knew all along and I was too scared to really do anything about it."

Now it was Mackenzie who sounded as if she were crying.

"What you wrote was beautiful."

"It was corny." Mackenzie sounded embarrassed. "I read all those romance novels I took from you in the hopes they would help me figure out something to say, and then I never got the courage to say it. Besides, you hated my guts by then."

"It's the most beautiful thing anyone has ever written to me."

"Colby, do you think—"

"Yes," Colby said.

"You don't even know what I'm going to ask," Mackenzie said, but there was relief in her voice.

"I always knew. The answer is yes. We'll find a way."

Mackenzie was so quiet for so long that Colby thought they had lost the connection. "Mackenzie, what are you doing?"

"I'm driving eighty-five miles an hour on Highway Five, looking for Sisters Road."

About the Author

Gabrielle Goldsby grew up in Oakland, California, where at the age of nine, she was left confined to her bed for weeks by a childhood illness. It was then, thanks to her mother's efforts to save her own sanity, that she discovered a love of reading. After receiving a bachelor's degree in criminal justice administration, she spent time as a gang and drugs prevention counselor, a flooring specialist for a large home improvement store, a facilities manager inside some of San Francisco's largest law firms, and an administrative assistant in the semiconductor industry. These varied occupations have become the basis for many past and future writing projects.

She is the 2008 Lambda Literary Award winner in mystery for *Wall of Silence*, 2nd ed., and the author of many other novels and short stories, including "The Player" in the all-romance anthology *Romantic Interludes 1: Discovery* from Bold Strokes Books.

Books Available From Bold Strokes Books

The Middle of Somewhere by Clifford Henderson. Eadie T. Pratt sets out on a road trip in search of a new life and ends up in the middle of somewhere she never expected. (978-1-60282-047-0)

Paybacks by Gabrielle Goldsby. Cameron Howard wants to avoid her old nemesis Mackenzie Brandt but their high school reunion brings up more than just memories. (978-1-60282-046-3)

Uncross My Heart by Andrews & Austin. When a radio talk show diva sets out to interview a female priest, the two women end up at odds and neither heaven nor earth is safe from their feelings. (978-1-60282-045-6)

Fireside by Cate Culpepper. Mac, a therapist, and Abby, a nurse, fall in love against the backdrop of friendship, healing, and defending one's own within the Fireside shelter. (978-1-60282-044-9)

Green Eyed Monster by Gill McKnight. Mickey Rapowski believes her former boss has cheated her out of a small fortune, so she kidnaps the girlfriend and demands compensation—just a straightforward abduction that goes so wrong when Mickey falls for her captive. (978-1-60282-042-5)

Blind Faith by Diane and Jacob Anderson-Minshall. When private investigator Yoshi Yakamota and the Blind Eye Detective Agency are hired to find a woman's missing sister, the assignment seems fairly mundane—but in the detective business, the ordinary can quickly become deadly. (978-1-60282-041-8)

A Pirate's Heart by Catherine Friend. When rare book librarian Emma Boyd searches for a long-lost treasure map, she learns the hard way that pirates still exist in today's world—some modern pirates steal maps, others steal hearts. (978-1-60282-040-1)

Trails Merge by Rachel Spangler. Parker Riley escapes the high-powered world of politics to Campbell Carson's ski resort—and their mutual attraction produces anything but smooth running. (978-1-60282-039-5)

Dreams of Bali by C.J. Harte. Madison Barnes worships work, power, and success, and she's never allowed anyone to interfere—that is, until she runs into Karlie Henderson Stockard. Eclipse EBook (978-1-60282-070-8)

The Limits of Justice by John Morgan Wilson. Benjamin Justice and reporter Alexandra Templeton search for a killer in a mysterious compound in the remote California desert. (978-1-60282-060-9)

Designed for Love by Erin Dutton. Jillian Sealy and Wil Johnson don't much like each other, but they do have to work together—and what they desire most is not what either of them had planned. (978-1-60282-038-8)

Calling the Dead by Ali Vali. Six months after Hurricane Katrina, NOLA Detective Sept Savoie is a cop who thinks making a relationship work is harder than catching a serial killer—but her current case may prove her wrong. (978-1-60282-037-1)

Dark Garden by Jennifer Fulton. Vienna Blake and Mason Cavender are sworn enemies—who can't resist each other. Something has to give. (978-1-60282-036-4)

Shots Fired by MJ Williamz. Kyla and Echo seem to have the perfect relationship and the perfect life until someone shoots at Kyla—and Echo is the most likely suspect. (978-1-60282-035-7)

truelesbianlove.com by Carsen Taite. Mackenzie Lewis and Dr. Jordan Wagner have very different ideas about love, but they discover that truelesbianlove is closer than a click away. Eclipse EBook (978-1-60282-069-2)

Justice at Risk by John Morgan Wilson. Benjamin Justice's blind date leads to a rare opportunity for legitimate work, but a reckless risk changes his life forever. (978-1-60282-059-3)

Run to Me by Lisa Girolami. Burned by the four-letter word called love, the only thing Beth Standish wants to do is run for—or maybe from—her life. (978-1-60282-034-0)

Split the Aces by Jove Belle. In the neon glare of Sin City, two women ride a wave of passion that threatens to consume them in a world of fast money and fast times. (978-1-60282-033-3)

Uncharted Passage by Julie Cannon. Two women on a vacation that turns deadly face down one of nature's most ruthless killers—and find themselves falling in love. (978-1-60282-032-6)

Night Call by Radclyffe. All medevac helicopter pilot Jett McNally wants to do is fly and forget about the horror and heartbreak she left behind in the Middle East, but anesthesiologist Tristan Holmes has other plans. (978-1-60282-031-9)

I Dare You by Larkin Rose. Stripper by night, corporate raider by day, Kelsey's only looking for sex and power, until she meets a woman who stirs her heart and her body. (978-1-60282-030-2)

Truth Behind the Mask by Lesley Davis. Erith Baylor is drawn to Sentinel Pagan Osborne's quiet strength, but the secrets between them strain duty and family ties. (978-1-60282-029-6)

Lake Effect Snow by C.P. Rowlands. News correspondent Annie T. Booker and FBI Agent Sarah Moore struggle to stay one step ahead of disaster as Annie's life becomes the war zone she once reported on. Eclipse EBook (978-1-60282-068-5)

Revision of Justice by John Morgan Wilson. Murder shifts into high gear, propelling Benjamin Justice into a raging fire that consumes the Hollywood Hills, burning steadily toward the famous Hollywood Sign—and the identity of a cold-blooded killer. (978-1-60282-058-6)

Cooper's Deale by KI Thompson. Two would-be lovers and a decidedly inopportune murder spell trouble for Addy Cooper, no matter which way the cards fall. (978-1-60282-028-9)

Romantic Interludes 1: Discovery ed. by Radclyffe and Stacia Seaman. An anthology of sensual, erotic contemporary love stories from the best-selling Bold Strokes authors. (978-1-60282-027-2)

Remember Tomorrow by Gabrielle Goldsby. Cees Bannigan and Arieanna Simon find that a successful relationship rests in remembering the mistakes of the past. (978-1-60282-026-5)